Original Irish Stories

60 Lyrical Yarns

by

Pat Watson

ISBN 0-9552496-0-0

9 780955 249600 >

First published 2006 by WEP - West Erin Publishing

Copyright Pat Watson 2006

The moral right of the author has been asserted.

A CIP catalogue of this book is available from the British Library.

Published by WEP - West Erin Publishing
Creagh, Bealnamulla, Athlone, Co. Roscommon, Ireland.
Web: www.myirishstories.com

Printed by Brosna Press, Ferbane. 090 6454327

Original Irish Stories
60 Lyrical Irish Glories
Ancient Times and New,
Nostalgic, funny or true.

Dedication

To Evelyn, my wife of forty-three years
And my best friend since 1958.

Special thanks for encouragement and assistance to all my family, Patricia and Michael, Brendan and Úna, Fiona and Damien, also Brian Lenihan, Georoid O'Brian, Fred Carney, Grace Brennan and all at Shannonside Northern Sound Radio, particularly the listeners who asked for this book.

Contents

A Paraffin Oil Table Lamp

"Please to help me Herr Mister, my bicycle she is punctured." Willie Killion was mesmerised. During the war, forty-year-old West of Ireland farmers' sons seldom met film-star types in distress while cycling to town. In her little saddlebag she had a full repair kit including two little tyre levers. Willie had always used spoons to remove tyres. The levers were much better, even if he was a bit addled by the strange fragrance. Perfume was rare in the west. She was talkative with the face and gait of a young girl; the body of a woman and a neck just like his mother. Judging by her hair she was a dab hand with the rack (comb). By the time the bicycle was back on its wheels he was enchanted.

She had just arrived in Ireland to escape the war. She was renting Carter's vacant house just here. She had lost everything, including her family.

"Would he like some tea? The kettle was on the boil". He stood in the sitting room holding his cap in his hand while she talked from the kitchen. "You to join me on the chaise longue," she said as she placed the tray on a little table. He had been looking at the sofa with only one end.

"So that's what it's called!" She sat on the reclining end while he gingerly sat on the other end. The tray had two cups and a plate with two little long loaves, split down the middle with sausages in the centre. Frankfurters, she called them. They were like rubber sausages, took a lot of chewing. He was on his way to town to buy the makings of a new suit. She would go with him.

As they cycled he forgot Mary, with her farm and her aging parents. For years she had been his best hope as his older brother was the heir apparent to the home farm. Not that he had got any farther than thinking of Mary. But this foreign lady stirred his fancy in a way totally new to him. She had said her name was Brigitte. He supposed that was a mispronounced Bridget! Sure Bridget was his mother's name. The parish church was St Bridget's; they even had a St Bridget's Holy Well. Was it a sign?

They parked their bicycles in the alley between the drapers and the hardware shop.

"Isn't zat lamp ze most beautiful lamp you ever saw!" she said, looking in the window.

"It would ve just perfect on my sitting room table! No? Ve had one just like it before ve lost everything. It would make life in this strange country just like ze Fatherland, but of course I can never have it, I am too poor now." She whimpered. As he looked at her sad face, she flashed her very long eyelashes. He never saw eyelashes that long before. The poor girl was distraught. The lamp was thirty-seven shillings and six pence. He had fifty shillings for the makings of the suit. If he bought her the lamp it would make her happy, she would smile again, it would make her forget her troubles and her loneliness, she would be very pleased and grateful, maybe very, very grateful. To hell with the suit, he would buy her the lamp.

They packed it in a wooden box, filling the inside of the globe with newspaper and packing the whole thing in fine sawdust. They even included a bottle of paraffin oil for fuel. Wasn't he the proud man cycling home with the luxury lamp on the carrier and the beautiful lady beside him. He wouldn't call the queen his aunt. It didn't bother him that she spoke friendly to an army fellow.

He unpacked the lamp, placed it on the table and when he fitted the globe it was magnificent.

"Vell Herr Villy Villian you are vonderful," she said and throwing out her arms, she caught him by the ears and kissed him lightly on the lips. His heart went mad. He was transfixed with a hideous grin. He had never been kissed before.

"Thank you velly, velly much Herr Villy," she said as she ushered him out the door.

"You must visit again, but now I have some letters to write." He jumped on the bike, emitting little yahoo's; sure he nearly did himself an injury jumping on the saddle. Night had fallen but with light in his heart he scarcely noticed. He could still feel where her lips met his. He could still smell the perfume. His ears would never be the same again. He pulled up suddenly. A thought had just struck him.

Why did she usher him out?

Had she expected him to respond to the kiss? Maybe she was disappointed. He should have guzzled her.

"You're a fool," he told himself.

"You waited a lifetime for this and now you're cycling away when you should be making hay." He turned back. He would return and take up where they left off. He was sure that's what she wanted.

What excuse would he give for coming back?

The box! He would say he wanted the box for a clucking hen, to set a clutch of eggs for hatching. That sounded plausible. Anyhow she would probably fly into his arms and words would be superfluous. After that he could play it by ear. He was very excited. Wasn't this his lucky day?

"It's night you idiot, day or night what matter? Go man go."

When he got to her house the blind was pulled and there was a man's bicycle outside. He went down on one knee and peeped in under the blind. Bridget was reclining in the chaise longue. The army fellow was reclining with her. He had his head left on her chest looking up at her. She was holding a frankfurter in her mouth and he was trying to bite it. He couldn't because she was holding his ears. He rapped on the door. She opened it. He brushed past her, took the lamp in both hands and walked out, his anger carrying him on.

"But Herr Villy ve vill have no light!"

"Ye won't need light for what you're at!"

Writing letters, my foot! To whom? Wasn't all belonging to her dead? "Moryagh".

She was probably a German spy. She was using her sausage to get information out of the army fellow. He hoped she'd get caught. They might even shoot her. She would roast in hell. It would be the price of her for meddling with the makings of a man's suit.

Half a mile down the road he came to Mary's house. He marched up the path still holding the lighted lamp. Mary looked out the window.

"Daddy! There's an apparition coming up the garden." The father looked out.

"Come Nancy," he said to his wife,

"Out the back door, this is a man on a mission, leave him to Mary." Mary opened the door. Willie marched in and put the lamp on the table. Mary held out her arms in awe. Before she could catch his ears he bear hugged her. She was agreeably surprised. She had been a little concerned about his masculinity, she need not have worried, he was all man. Even the old couple peeping in the window squeezed hands.

Did they all live happily ever after? Why wouldn't they? Hadn't they the best-lit parlour in the parish!

Cheeky Boy

He had waited for this day all his life. Now he had his chance. He would show them. For years, in fact all his life they had been belittling and making a joke of him. Why, even his father sometimes seemed to forget his existence. Only today his brothers had verbally abused him and called him a cheeky brat. Now was his chance to show them up and he would not fail.

He had only been brought on as a sub and the very last sub at that. He was not in their first team or even their second team, nor was he on the bench, why he was not even in the crowd, but now he was on the field, here in the valley. This was his big chance, the chance of a lifetime. He would not blow it. He would prove his mettle to himself and everybody else. He must keep his cool and yet play the fool. He had the ability, he had the nerve, he had the knowledge. His own modern technology would win the day. He was fitter and stronger than anyone thought. He had been running twenty miles each way to play gigs for VIPs. He was fit and fast, he had strength and stamina. He had courage and determination, he had sex appeal. Boy had he sex appeal! He had fought bears before, fought and won. He had groupies around the gigs he played. But after today every girl in the country would desire him. And would he enjoy that? Would he what! He would not leave them longing. It would drive his big brothers wild. This would not just make him equal to his brothers; it would make him totally superior. Then, he would get his own back for today's humiliation, indeed for a lifetime of humiliation. His hairy adversary was still some distance away. He could swagger and sing for a while yet. He must look soft, silly even simple. To lull his opponent into a false sense of security. That was his plan. Those were fearsome roars, he was getting madder, bide your time boy, keep it cool, he was coming straight this way. Now is the moment, both feet firmly on the ground. Cheeky Boy now chose his roundest water honed projectile for least wind drag. He took cool and careful aim. He let fly. Plonk, he hit the mighty creature right in the middle of the forehead. For a second he swayed backward then fell forward flat on his face. With a leap and a bound Cheeky Boy was upon him, lifting the great sword and cutting off his head. He held the great hairy head aloft, the hot blood spattering his bare legs. There was a gasp from the crowd and in the second's silence that followed Cheeky Boy called out, "henceforth I will be known by my own name. David."

Christmas Love

He was foot loose and fancy free, he had come home from England this Christmas Eve with enough money to cut a dash with the neighbours. Just for Christmas he would have a ball, then back to the bright lights of London. That's what he told everyone but London could be a cold place, flatland was no Utopia. He had got no sleep on the boat, The Princess Maud, last night but his time was short and he had to make the most of it. He could sleep tonight. Next year he would go to America. But for one last week he would enjoy the craic in Ireland of the nineteen fifties.

Then it happened, she just walked by, was she real? Nobody moved like that. Was she on wheels? No, she moved on the most beautiful legs, sort of glided, as only one with a perfect shape could.

"Don't just stand there, follow her," he told himself. The friends from whom he excused himself looked on in amusement. He has it bad, one of them said.

As he followed a thought struck him, what would he say when he caught up to her? He couldn't ask if she was real. He couldn't just say, "You are beautiful." Maybe he would just scare her. He had to think of something. He didn't get the chance. She turned into the Friary Church. He followed her. She joined the queue for confession. He joined the queue for confession beside her. When somebody came behind him it gave him an excuse to move in close to her. Their shoulders touched. Their hips touched, their knees touched. He was glad the queue was long and the priest slow. He could go on like this indefinitely, moving on to sit where she had just sat, feeling her warmth, listening to her breathing and generally feeling comfortable in her aura. All too soon her turn came and she disappeared into the confessional.

He listened hard but could hear nothing. As she came out, he stood up to go in. She stood in his way. He moved to the right. She moved to the right. He moved to the left. She moved to the left, nearly like dancing. He looked down at her. She looked up at him, slightly blushing, a hint of a glint, a trace of a Mona Lisa smile a foursome of freckles on a tiny turned up nose and overall heart stopping beauty. No man should be feeling like this going to confession. Then she spoke with a heavenly husky voice more mature than her teenage body." The priest says he is not hearing anymore, go to the next confessional." He turned and did her bidding.

By the time he got out she was gone. He searched the church, he searched the bicycle park, he searched outside but all to no avail. She was nowhere to be seen. Was she real or had he been hallucinating? He thought he had reached Nirvana, that they would talk for hours, that she would feel the same as him but now nothing only a cold winter's night. Was he being punished for falling in love in church when he should have being praying? Probably. He would pray at Midnight Mass. He might as well become a monk if he could not find this apparition again.

The church was magnificent, full of light, of life, of music and packed with people but no sign of his fantasy girl. The choir was singing "Adeste Fideles". There was a sort of magic nostalgia about the whole scene, "natum videte regem angelorum," but no sign of his fantasy girl. "Venite adoremus." It was glorious, "Dominum." Had he really seen her or had the lack of sleep addled his mind? Maybe she was pure imagination as nobody could be that beautiful, still no sign of her. With glory, pomp, pageantry and ceremony they finally got through the Mass, now the final hymn.

Silent night, holy night, should that be lonely night? The solo singer was enchanting. All is calm, all is bright, too calm and not so bright. As the multitude slowly made their way out he looked all around but she was nowhere to be found. "Sleep in heavenly peace, sleep in heavenly peace". He certainly needed the sleep but would he ever be at peace again?

At last he spotted her outside the church with an older lady. She had been watching him and when their eyes met her face lit up with the most dazzling smile totally eclipsing even the vision in his mind.

"Mammy" she said, "this is the boy I told you about, may I bring him home for breakfast?"

All his Christmases had come together. He never saw London again.

Mother Moore
and her Summerhill Drainage Gang

Her vocation was to serve, to care for one child or another
But fate just intervened and she wound up Reverend Mother.
When a legacy came to her, a vow of poverty she'd made
She could not take the money; she had a problem it was said.
Then she had a great idea, a vision if you will
She'd use up all the money to drain old Summerhill.

It was in the hungry thirties and the peasantry was poor,
She'd pay them well for digging, this wonder Mother Moore.
And while they did the digging she'd teach them how to pray,
They'd get salvation, education and a half a crown a day.
She did her own recruiting, twelve strong young men and true,
Neither jury nor apostles, but a good hard working crew.

Paddy Dwyer and Bill Colleran were half the men from Drum,
Christy Jarrett and James Lennon made up the full foursome.
Cornafulla's Jack McManus and Pa Colleran, Kielty's man
With all the rest from Crannagh, I'll name them if I can.
Sonny Donlon, Richard Higgins, and Jack Harney all were there,
Mickey Murray, Patrick Harney and Tom Curley of red hair.

Two of those men were carters, who got an extra bob a day
Mickey Murray and Jack Harney, they drew all the stuff away.
Mickey Murray had a jennet, Big Jack a clydesdale mare

They both received a shilling; Jack said it wasn't fair.
But the Mother interjected, "Don't crib about the pay,
It was a cousin of the jennet, our Saviour rode Palm Day."

They started work at eight; each answered the roll call
Christy Jarrett led the prayers; answered fervently by all.
And when the prayer was ended; the Mother she would say
I want an honest day of work for the honest way I pay.
The mother she would urge them, to work with all their will
And sometimes she would call, work faster, faster still.

On the south side of the building, at the entrance to the school
What was once a cool spring pond was now a stagnant pool.
To get this water flowing, round to the bull field drain
A trench they'd have to dig, through very rough terrain.
Full five feet deep and four feet wide, they'd have to dig this drain
Worked by just tools of hand, with muscle brawn and strain.

The gravel was rock hard, the boulders tons in weight
Yet progress fast was made the effort was so great.
From eight to twelve each day, there was neither stop nor stay,
Till twelve bells gave the summons, to wipe their brow's and pray.
They prayed with great devotion, slow, reverend and devout,
For men who are work weary, will stretch the least timeout.

They worked in every weather, rain, frost or snow or sun
Yet not a single day was missed by Mother Moore the nun.
When falling stone crushed big Jack's toe he winced in searing pain
And uttered words so loud and clear and just somewhat profane.
Then Mother said, "Hell waits for those who utter words like that."
Jack muttered low beneath his breath, "Sure hell is where we're at."

When standing on the bank one day, above the toiling men
The earth gave way beneath her feet and she just tumbled in.
Pat Harney then and Sonny rushed up to give her aid
Imagine then their great surprise when Reverend Mother said,
"Just hand me here the ladder and don't you stand about"
Though dirty wet and injured, she quickly clambered out.

At last they got the great drain dug, and water flowed so free,
They lined it all with large flagstones; it was a sight to see.
And ever since it worked so well that all the yard stayed dry,
And children play and skip around and never once think why.
Now that the group have all aspired, to heaven's sweet refrain,
I wonder if they think at all of Summerhill's "auld" drain.

Patrick Donnellan who was known as "Sonny Donlon" told this story.
And he was the last survivor of the group when he died in 1998.
Larry Donlon, who was a brother of Sonny, lived on to 2003. In the last months of
his life in a Nursing Home, he had this poem read to him daily. He would always
say "Read it again."

Generation Gap

Dear old Summerhill with your hills and your dells
Your men of tomorrow will never wield flails

Instead they drive autos, devices propelled,
By mechanical power and in speed unexcelled.

They work in the town and in money abound
And all through the day you hear not a sound.

But when Angelus chimes on this fair land once more
Our workers come home with clamber galore.

For from then to the dawn you are likely to hear,
All the lads and the lassies in merry good cheer.

For those lads have a strong flair, a flair for fair maids
And the lassies love likewise their charming young aids.

Though livestock's neglected and chores stay undone
Young love will prevail and the race will go on.

A Different Drum

Around the end of the war we were in third class. The class consisted of about thirty, nine-to-ten year olds and about ten dunces of various ages and sizes who sat down the back. These had been kept back, denied promotion to higher classes, because it was felt that another year in the same grade, would bring them up to speed. Very slow learners might spend two years in every class from infants up and as a result might finish school in third class.

Fitz was the biggest dunce in every respect. He was six feet tall and weighed ten stone. He sat on a stool at the end, as he would not fit in the desk seat. He never knew anything, in fact nobody ever heard him say anything in class. Occasionally the master would ask him a spelling or a sum but Fitz would never reply. The master would hit him a few belts and move on to the next pupil. Fitz never complained or seemed annoyed about being beaten or called a dunce. In the playground he just stood around, ate his lunch quietly and didn't say very much. Any boy being chased by a bully could find sanctuary in his shadow.

Then one day Fitz hit out at Slasher, the next biggest dunce. The master was on the scene in a flash.

"Fitz, this is not like you, why did you hit Slasher?"

"He spilled me "tae" ration into me sugar ration."

"And why have you your tea and sugar in school?"

"Sure the stepmother would eat them and feed them to her young ones if I left them at home."

"In future leave his rations alone. How old are you Fitz?"

"I'll be fourteen tomorrow Sir."

"When are you leaving school?"

"Today Sir." This was the first time we ever heard Fitz speak in class; even the master was surprised.

Then the master did a funny thing.

"I will never give out to you or punish you again but I want you to do just one thing for me on this your last day at school." He brought him up to the board and wrote 2 with another 2 under it and a line under that again.

"Can you do that sum for me?" he said.

As far as we were concerned the plus sign had not been invented. Fitz said nothing.

"Just tell me if you don't know the answer, I won't say anything to you."

"I don't know," said Fitz.

"O dear! O dear!" said the master "we have failed you, what are you going to do in life?"

"I start work tomorrow with Tom Smith, sorting spuds."

"But he will fool you. If he promises you two shillings an hour for an eight-hour day, you won't know how much to expect."

"Sixteen bob" said Fitz. The master just smiled and said,

"Good luck to you in life Fitz; we have been marching to a different drum."

The God of Comfort

There was once a king who ruled over a great country and all his subjects were reasonably happy. However, he always had a problem trying to provide enough money to run his castle, his court, his army and his wife and at the same time, appear to be generous to the poor. Although he was a king he was well aware that it was always easier to lead with a carrot than drive with a stick, hence his preoccupation with money. There seemed to be resistance to every type of tax no matter how fair he thought it was. As for the poor, their needs could never be met. If he could only find a tax that his subjects would willingly pay.

Then one day the king had a vision. He was visited by a funny looking little man who said he was the god of comfort. The little man said to the king, "I could be a great comfort to you, to all in your household, and indeed to all your people throughout your kingdom. And the wonderful part is that at the same time I can greatly increase your take from taxes with no resistance or criticism from anywhere. Why, you could have a richer court, a better army, a more amiable wife and still have enough left for the poor."

"That sounds wonderful," said the king.

"You must really be a god. How can we ever pay you back? Will we have to pray more? Or do penance? Or wear sackcloth and ashes? Or will you require a blood sacrifice?"

"The latter," said the little man, which greatly alarmed the king.

"What sort of sacrifice?"

"Around three hundred people a year."

"What do you mean, three hundred people a year?"

"I mean I will take three hundred of your people every year just as your

God takes all your people in the end anyhow."

"Ah, these will be old people whose lives are already spent."

"Oh no, they will be people of every age picked at random, at a time and place of my choosing."

"They will be all from the poor and disabled."

"No, no, they will be from any family I choose, perhaps even yours."

"That is preposterous," said the king.

"I will never agree to it, my people will never agree. Why, our God would send a plague on us if we agreed to such a thing."

"I promise you that your God will not send a plague unless you ask him for one, but just let me talk to the people and if they are satisfied with the deal, will you go along with them?"

"Ask away, but they will turn you down just as I have."

"Do we have a deal then?"

"Not unless you get full agreement with no dissent,"

"To get no dissent is impossible, you know that, I know that, everybody knows that. Why nobody who ever did anything worthwhile in this world got away without some criticism. Would you be satisfied if there was only one person in five critical?"

"It would have to be less than one in ten," said the king knowing that support of that level could never be achieved.

"If I get this level of agreement then, you will not object?"

The king thought about the extra taxes, about the comfort for himself, his wife, and his household, and his subjects would be compliant if they had their say.

"Deal," he said and shook the little man's hand.

The little man first addressed the middle aged.

"You have worked hard all of your humdrum lives, you have done reasonably well for yourselves, your families and your country but you never got proper recognition for your efforts. Your lives are slipping away, most of your best days are gone and now initiative and power are passing to the young. Are you to be remembered as the generation of no achievement?

However, if you now come and worship at my shrine all that will change, change utterly. People will look up to you, starting with your neighbours and spreading to people throughout the land. Even strangers will salute you. You will have a whole new status in life. You will feel in control for the first time in your lives. You will be able to decide your own future direction, and not be led by somebody else as heretofore. Even your own children will want to go places with you, to be seen with you, to say to their friends, there go my parents. Compete with that if you can, they will say."

"That sounds great, but where's the snag? What will the cost be?"

"Well," said the little man, "there will be a reasonable monitory cost but that's only to be expected and I don't suppose anybody will object." There was an occasional little rumble here and there among the listeners but they were quickly eliminated by sharp remarks and even sharper looks from the liberals.

"There is also the three hundred people a year which I will require," said the little man. "What do you mean three hundred people a year?" they asked.

"What do you want them for?"

"I will take them to my kingdom in the next world when they die at a time and place of my choosing."

At this there was uproar among the people.

"Are you mad? We would never agree to that, in fact nobody would even consider such a ridiculous suggestion."

Then somebody said,

"We should not have totally closed minds. Everything is worth discussing if only for academic reasons. First, let us establish what exactly the man means."

"I mean, that I must be entirely free to take any person I like at any time I like and in return, you can have all the good things I promised and more. And remember, all those people will die eventually whether you agree or not."

At this, the liberals took heart and suggested that most of those chosen would probably be strangers from the far end of the country.

"More than likely, we would not even know them or anybody belonging to them" they said.

"After all, three hundred out of three million is only one in ten thousand.

Sure, several people would be expected to die out of ten thousand anyhow and would one more make any difference? If three score and ten is the average life span then one in seventy must enter and leave this life annually. If one in ten thousand was to leave a little early it would not make any difference to the average, and indeed the one in question might even be seventy years or more and in that case we would be actually gaining." Some more conservative people suggested that this was confused waffle but when challenged, they could not agree among themselves or produce a coherent and convincing spokesman.

Again the liberals came forward,

"We cannot stand in the way of progress," they said, "we must not forever be stuck in the mud. We must keep up with the rest of the world; we owe that much to our children and to future generations. Opportunities like this don't come every day; we may never get this chance again. Are we losers or what?" Again there were mutterings from the conservatives,

"Let the silent majority have their say," they said, but the silent majority remained silent as they always do.

"We must not be railroaded into this as we have been railroaded into every new and shady scheme that comes along."

"Ah, so you admit that you are against progress from any quarter?"

"That is not what we said," they whimpered, but the initiative was lost to them, they said no more, they never thought that the deal would be agreed. The loud mouths had hogged the debate but they still had no hope of a nine to one majority. Common sense would prevail.

Satisfied with that debate the little man now turned his attention to the young men.

"To all who idolize me," he said, "I will give power, prestige, daring and panache. You will be the pride of your parents, the envy of your friends and the darlings of your adoring grandparents. You will have power, far, far greater than any young people who ever lived in this world. Your freedom will seem unlimited. You will feel invincible. You will have courage beyond your wildest dreams. You will be enabled to outdo bigger stronger opponents. Nobody, but nobody will be able to bully you. In fact you will not feel beholden to God or man. Young ladies will seek you out, will desire your company and will just want to be with you. On many occasions they may ask you out or request that you escort them home or even take them on holiday. Imagine such changes to your life. Now are you prepared to sacrifice the three hundred?"

"We are, we are," they said,

"If you got to go, you got to go, and if you only half live, why bother?"

Having watched the enthusiastic acceptance by the young men the conservatives became a little alarmed but they felt confident that the young girls would more than offset any ground lost. After all they were well reared young women, nurtured by careful caring mothers and educated by sober and dedicated teachers. They would send the smooth talking little man away with a flea in his ear. Unlike the fickle young men who had always disliked discipline, their girls would mirror the moral mores of their mentors. He would see that not everybody in this society was a simple soul. He could never win now.

Turning to the young girls the little god said, "If you will worship me, I promise to whisk you away on the trip of a lifetime. You will be charmed, thrilled, exhilarated, carried away on the wings of wonder, to romance, to love, to dreams come true. Never before in the history of the world have women known such feelings. Now they are yours for the asking. Are you prepared to risk the three hundred? Remember, any one of you may be chosen."

"When do we start?" they shrieked.

At this turn of events the conservatives were extremely alarmed and they pleaded with the king to get rid of the little impostor, to banish him from the country and to restore normality. The king listened to their pleas and considered their case. Then he summoned the little man.

"Now look here," he said, "I am the king here and I will call the shots."

"Does that mean you mean to break our deal?"

"I will break it if I wish, but that won't be necessary as you do not have the support of nine out of ten, as we agreed."

"It does not matter now for nobody will object except some old fogies who don't matter anyhow. The people will insist on pandering to me now, no matter what you or anybody else say or do. They are mine now."

This greatly annoyed the king.

"Just who are you?" said he angrily,

"What is your real name?"

At this the little man wiped his shining brow with a pristine handkerchief and said,

"My name is Motorcar."

The Bar of his Bike

The bar of a fellow's bike was a very intimate place to be. The saying goes "come to live with me if you want to know me" but the next best thing is to get on the bar of his bike. With his hands on the handlebars and his feet on the pedals and he overlooking your head, he has you cocooned within his aura as it were. You might be just two of a group making their way home and you might be in conversation with everyone else, but all this takes place from within the confines of his cocoon and is therefore seen as much through his eyes as your own. Others too, see you in a different light. A would be suitor may see you as taken, or spoken for, or at least compromised and not available. What about him?

What is he thinking? Does he think he owns me? Does he feel a bit giddy like me? How does he feel about being this near? Does he feel it is comfortable or dangerous or a bit of both? I notice he is breathing hard, is he carried away or excited or just getting it hard to push? If I look back up at him will it seem cheeky? How near will our faces be or will he kiss me? What would it be like? Would I enjoy it? Would he? Go for it. Oh no I couldn't. I couldn't bear rejection. Maybe he just thinks I'm heavy and that the journey will never end. All this talk by everyone about what happened at the dance is clouding the issue. I wish they would shut up and let us have a private conversation. What would we say? What would we do? Why is he scratching my head with his chin? Now he's nibbling my ear, the others have gone on ahead, I think I'll look back up at him now. I hope we don't fall off the bike. Who cares?

The Thirty Two Counties

Chorus
There are thirty-two counties in Ireland
All named in this lyrical rhyme.
For the Gaels they have lived in old Ireland
Since the very beginning of time.

We have Leitrim Fermanagh and Cavan,
Roscommon Mayo and Galway
And those counties are like unto heaven
But the emigrants still go away.

Chorus

In the east we have Louth Meath and Dublin
In the south we have Cork and Kerry,
With Limerick and Clare by the Shannon
And up by Tyrone is Derry.

Chorus

Wicklow is land of sweet beauty
Offaly is Saint Kieran's rest,
Monaghan's the town of the duty
But dear Down I love it the best.

Chorus

We have Carlow, Kilkenny and Longford
Antrim Armagh and Kildare
Waterford and Sligo and Wexford
And sweet Tipperary so fair.

Chorus

Westmeath is right in the middle,
Laois was once called the Queen
Now to end the thirty-two riddle,
Donegal has landscapes serene.

Chorus

The Woman on the High Nellie Bicycle

Mary and John were finishing their breakfast when there she was, standing in the open doorway of their farmhouse kitchen.

"Does Michael Joseph Kelly of Clooneen Mór live here?" That was her opening remark.

"And good morning to you too" said Mary,

"And who's asking?"

"I must speak to Michael Joseph, is he here?"

"No he's gone since early morning."

"When will he be back?"

"Not until late tonight".

"I'll wait", she said as she sat in the chair inside the door.

"What do you want with him?"

"It's private, between him and me."

"But we're his parents, surely you can tell us."

"I will not divulge anything."

"But you can't stay here all day and not tell us what you want with Mike."

"I'll wait."

"Not in here?"

"I'll wait outside so," and she stood up.

"Stay where you are, enough people have you seen already." After that silence fell.

Up to now Mary had done all the talking. John, who never had much to say, was weighing up the situation. First he thought that this woman was here on her own behalf, after all, their Mike was a hot-blooded young fellow. "Na", it was years since she saw forty and she was thin as a whip, pinched even. Her high Nellie bicycle, which he could see out the window, was pre war, possibly twenty years old. Not even a hot blooded twenty year old could do anything for her. It must be her daughter, but she had no wedding ring. Maybe she was an aunt, a maiden aunt with some sort of profession, a poultry instructress or something of the sort. If so he hoped the niece would be better looking and not as sour. He knew Mary was thinking the same thing. She didn't get far with the questions. He would have a go.

"Did you come far?"

"Far enough."

"How did you find the way?"

"I asked."

"Who did you ask?"

"A nice woman, said her name was Kate, she came two miles out of her way to show me."

"And asked plenty of questions I'll wager?"

"She did."

"And did you tell her your business?"

"Only that I was looking for Michael Joseph."

"Did ye meet many?"

"A few."

"And did they speak to ye?"

"Kate told them who I was looking for."

Glory be to God thought Mary, did she have to meet the greatest gabby gut in the parish, and to cycle two miles with her, the whole country will have it by now and we still don't know. They must find out. She had been too sharp. She would try again.

"Will you have a cup of tea"?

"No thanks."

"Ah go on it's in the pot."

"Alright so." She downed the tea and two buttered scones. She didn't look comfortable.

"Will you come out to the henhouse with me to look for eggs?"

"No" she said, stone faced.

"Are you sure." The penny dropped, the eyes softened, both women knew that there was no toilet in the house.

"I will so." Mary felt that a woman-to-woman talk especially in a compromising position would bring information but all she got was,

"That's a great relief."

"Can you not just tell me, I won't let on I know anything?"

"Only Michael Joseph."

"Well can you give me a hint?"

"No it's between him and me." So much for that approach.

The day wore on in the same vein. Between silences Mary and John took turns at questioning but all to no avail. They had dinner, they had evening tea, and they took another trip to the henhouse, but still to no avail. She would not budge. Finally they heard Mike coming in the lorry. Nobody moved until he came into the kitchen.

She stood up smartly and asked?

"Are you Michael Joseph Kelly of Clooneen Mor?"

"I am." Whereupon she took an official looking envelope out of her pocket and handed it him. He looked at the envelope. He looked again at the bearer, from her face to her toes and back again to her face. Mary wondered what was he thinking. Was he wondering could I have been that drunk? He opened the envelope. As he read his face reddened, then he guffawed.

"Is that all you want? Look Mother, it's only a summons for driving over some private property and you thought! Ah it serves you right." They all laughed with relief.

"Thanks for the tea, the henhouse, the dinner, the tea and the henhouse," she said as she sailed off on her high Nellie.

Seven Churches

The ramblers in our house used to tell of the great patrons of Seven Churches. Seven Churches was the local name for Clonmacnoise, which, although only about eight miles away, was in a different parish, a different diocese, a different county, a different province and the other side of the river Shannon in what the old people called The Kings County. Yet we knew all about the goings on there, on patron Sunday, the Sunday nearest the ninth of September, the great gathering of young people, the trick-of-the-loops, the three card trick men, various sellers of artefacts, religious and otherwise, the occasional frog thrown on to gaming tables or to unwelcoming girls, and the whispering arch.

In the fifteenth century, Dean Odo Malone installed a very elaborate cut-stone doorframe in the north door of the cathedral. This frame has seven or eight, sort of half pipes, cut into the stone, right around the arch and they can clearly carry a whisper all the way round to the other side. They will not carry a voice. My mother often told of half a dozen girls on one side whispering to a similar number of boys on the other side. The problem was that you could never be sure who would pick up your message, as you had to lean right into the arch. The people on the other side held their ears to the arch and they could see the speakers. I suppose it was the texting of the time. "How would you like to be buried with my people?" Or "The back of your head is looking good." A genuine marriage proposal made here carried great luck. The snag was that different pipes carried different blessings, such as a large family, a small family, mostly boisterous boys, all girls or a priest in the family and other things best not talked about. Nobody knew which was which, but the good outnumbered the bad.

It seemed that the pipe with the large family was mostly used, as nearly all families were large then. Perhaps it was the middle one that carried the whisper the clearest or maybe it made a difference whether it was the man or the woman who initiated the whisper. Some people thought it was the colour of the hair of the second speaker but that could not be right either as families were large regardless. However one thing was certain, no whisperers wound up alone! The arch is still there so if you fancy your chances, just go along and wait until a suitable looking partner is passing and whisper your piece.

Old Summerhill

An Explanation

The Seminary for the diocese of Elphin was originally founded at Summerhill, Athlone, which is two miles out the Ballinasloe road. This happened some time after Catholic Emancipation was achieved in 1829, mainly through the efforts of Daniel O'Connell, "The Liberator." He later addressed a great repeal meeting there in 1843. It's claimed there were half a million people present in the natural amphitheatre on the front lawn. The seminary was moved to Summerhill, Sligo circa 1880, hence the name Old Summerhill. It has been a centre of Catholic education in one form or another in all the years since 1829.

"Eureka" - Greek for, "I have it" which was the phrase immortalised by "Archimedes", the great Greek mathematician who discovered "that when a body is suspended in water it will float when the weight of the water disturbed is equal to the weight of the body."

"Veni,Vidi,Vice," Latin - "I came, I saw, I conquered", as said by Julius Caesar when reporting his victory over the king of Pontus to the Roman Senate.

"Viva", Italian--- Long live.

"Papyrus"- The first paper invented by the Egyptians.

"Quill"- feather writing pen.

Homer and Euclid- famous Greek scholars who helped to shape western society as it is today.

Ts'ai Lun- Old Chinese scholar who still influences the Chinese people who make up one fifth of the world population.

Sean Cnoc on tSamhraidh
Go hiontach, go halainn,
The past and the present
Are enriched by your calling.

Eureka said the Bishop
When first he saw your view
A seminary I'll build here
To train Gods chosen few.

Vene, vidi, vici
So said the Liberator
When out on your front lawn
For half-a-million he did cater.

Mar fuar se an ceadunas
In ochtdéag fiche naoi
To practise our religion
Openly and free.

Your position's in the centre
Of this land so green and quaint,
Your traditions bear the hallmark
Of the scholar and the saint.

Viva your dedication
Fighting ignorance and strife
For with modern education
You set youngsters up for life.

Your culture's one of knowledge
Based on papyrus and quill
Homer, Euclid and Ts'ai lun
Are revered in Summerhill.

Luas or the London Tube Train

Fifty years later we have the Luas, Ireland's answer to the London Tube Train. I don't understand a word that the four Polish lads in front of me are saying, but they look just like the four west of Ireland lads on the London tube train in nineteen fifty-five. They were talking about their ability to dig spuds with a spade, to drive pigs to the fair, and one of them claimed to be the best "slanesman" at digging turf in the West. I suppose the Poles were talking of something similar. They have the bogs, the pigs and the spuds and they looked like rural dwellers, so why not? There were no bogs in London then, just as there are no bogs in Dublin now. Like the Irish of old they work in construction. It may not be for McAlpine or Wimpey, but it's sure to be someone similar.

The driver calls out the next stop. The Four Courts, Ná Ceithre Cuirteanna. I thought for a minute he might say Camden Town or Tottenham Court Road. The young Chinese girl sitting opposite in the sunlight is talking on her mobile. Her over done lipstick is showing on her teeth as she laughs. Perhaps she comes from teeming Beijing but I prefer to think she is talking about the paddy-fields or the little terraced hillsides above the Yangtze River. Then again she may be ordering a take-away.

The two Nigerian women with the children on their backs speak perfect English. As they are wearing crucifixes round their necks, I suspect Irish Missionaries educated them or their parents or built their schools. They are talking about their jobs in an accountancy office. It's great to see them here. I hope they integrate happily into Irish society as good or better than the last generation did in London. The driver calls, Smithfield, Margadh Na Feirme. It used to be The Dublin Cattle Market. The young Irish couple getting off here told me they just bought an apartment for three hundred thousand euro. They have one room let to Lithuanians who pay half the mortgage. We Irish paid the Londoner's mortgages in the fifties.

The two Philippino nurses are probably on their way to Tallaght hospital or Saint James's. They remind me of Mary-Ann and Peggy who nursed in Guys in London. I wonder where are they now. Isn't it great the way nurses seem forever young? The Irish nurses used to be just "it". Now they are just "IT" people, hence the Philippine help who are now just "it". I hope the "IT" people appreciate the "it" people. The driver calls "The Museum, Ard Mhúsaem." The Londoners never said Baile An Camden or Bohar Na Tottenham Cuirteanna. They're all the poorer for that.

Isn't it grand the way you can see the sun, the rain and the scudding clouds through the windows of the Luas. One never saw anything only the dark dirty walls of the tube. You could dream of the bogs, the green hills or the wild mountains but there you were like a rat in a hole singing about when there's brighter days in Ireland. Well! The brighter days are here, as are all the immigrants including second and third generation Irish who emigrated in the last century. May they find the old Ireland that their ancestors dreamed about! The next stop is Hueston, connecting with all mainline rail lines to the country. Having crossed two countries we arrived at Euston main line station in London all those years ago. It's great to be back!

Liquid Stockings

For over a year now, Sheila had dreamed of getting silk stockings for her sixteenth birthday. Her mother had promised her. In spite of the war, in spite of the shortage of money, in spite of the ration books, she would have her silk stockings. But the war and the rations and the shortages won. Whatever few silk stockings got through to Ireland were mopped up by the big shots in Dublin. None were available for sixteen-year-old country girls. However, not to worry, there was a brand new alternative! Liquid stockings.

They came in a sort of hexagon jam-jar with instructions on the jar. You need a competent assistant and a small brush. Luckily they had a two-inch paintbrush. If they had to borrow one, the word might get about. Next, stand on newspaper in underwear with legs apart, tucking in any loose garments to avoid contamination. Get assistant to apply the liquid, starting above the knee at the garter level and working downward to the feet. Just lightly apply with a brush, taking particular care to get to the bottom of any creases behind the knees. Stay in position for twenty minutes to allow liquid to dry. The imitation seams down the back of the legs were put on with a pencil. She supposed, you have to suffer to be beautiful.

Her mother, Mary, was appointed as brush wielding assistant. She did a perfect job; not only in completing the liquid application but also in convincing Sheila that the whole project was worthwhile, that the stockings looked very real and that she would be the belle of the ball at the maypole that night. She was acutely aware that she had failed to get the real thing and she could only hope that this compromise would work. When Sheila did a twirl in the kitchen and said,

"How do you like my new silk stockings Daddy?" He looked out over his glasses and said, "In a whole jar full of instructions it never once mentions paint."

"Daddy" she said very cross, "That's because it's not paint, it's liquid silk stockings."

"Humm" was his reply.

The Maypole was an open-air dance held in a sheltered garden with a maple floor and the band playing in a sort of tree house. It ran Sundays and Thursdays throughout the summer. This was Thursday. After dark Paddy would hoist three carbide lamps on a clothesline above the hedge, the low disco lights of the time.

As Sheila and her friend Kitty walked the half mile to the dance, they passed by Mikey Joe's farm. Sheila and he had caught each other looking at each other a few times lately. Would he come to the maypole? Would he be impressed with her stockings? Would he dance with her? He was shearing sheep as they passed. Kitty noticed that they both spoke friendly, maybe a bit too friendly. She pretended not to notice. If he were coming he would be late as he had four more sheep to shear.

The dance was great for a while until it began to cloud over and the midges arrived. They seemed to be attracted to the stockings, the sheen, the slight odour or the colour. They could not bite through so they headed for higher ground to an area that no respectable girl could be seen scratching in public. Here they launched an all out attack. They were starving and apparently drunk to boot. They were having a ball. Not so Sheila, she was being bitten, stung, itched and tickled. She had to grin and bear it. The night was a disaster, worse was to come. As they danced the "feed of inions", that's what they called the Siege of Ennis, the rain came, a thick heavy mist. At least it got very dark and a girl could do a few unconventional steps and twists, murdering a few vicious midges in the process, but most of them clung on by the skin of their teeth.

Just as the dance ended, Paddy raised the lamps and threw a little light on the scene. Sheila looked down. Her stockings were dissolving with the rain, brown streaks on her black shoes, like - like you don't want to know. She looked over at Paddy. Mikey Joe was standing behind him wearing a hat and a long coat thrown over his shoulders. He was looking straight at her and her run-a-way stockings. She was mortified. If only the ground would open and swallow her. What was he doing? Pulling the loop off the clothesline. The carbide lamps fell on to the hedge and quenched, the darkness swallowed them up. There was some shouting and confusion. She felt a mantle envelope her and an arm. She looked up through the half-light. Mikey Joe was smiling down from under his hat.

"Can I walk you home?"

"Yes."

"We'll leave now before the lights are fixed."

An hour later, with the stockings washed off, the insect bites dabbed with disinfectant, she was sitting on her bed, puckering her lips and practising her smile in the mirror.

This had been a tumultuous day in her young life. She had got her longed-for blooming stockings. She had cut a dash for an hour. Then she had been tortured tickled, teased, tasted, terrified and traumatised. She had been rescued by her hero, walked home under his coat and his big strong arm, kissed, told she was beautiful and kissed again. Life was good. She was in love.

All Gone

It's lonely now round Daly's Mill,
For all have gone away.
It's lonely now round Daly's Mill,
This is a dreary day.

There's Johnny, Billy, Jack and Tom,
They work in Birmingham.
Young Noreen's gone to London town,
John-Joe is in Siam.

Wee Frank they called the cricket man
Now plays with a Scottish band
And Peggy, Jane and Maryann
Toil in Mississippi Land.

Young Jimmy died in the Philippines,
He was a priest of God.
Our Mary joined the nuns at home
But now she's gone abroad.

The Sweeney's from the hills above
Have gone across the sea.
The cooing of that lonesome dove
Shakes every nerve in me.

It's lonely now round Daly's Mill,
For all have gone away.
It's lonely now round Daly's Mill
And I alone must stay.

Will Ye Come, Jackeens Come?

Oh come civil servants from Dublin to live,
In Carrick, Roscommon or Cavan.
You'll find that the prices that you'll have to give,
Are very much less than you're having.
Your three-bedroom semi in Dublin will buy,
Five beds and some land for a pony.
And the saving from idling in traffic oh my,
Will leave you with plenty of money.
Now Cavan has trout lakes in every square mile,
The source of the Erne and the Shannon,
And you'll always be met with a genuine smile
All the way from Lough Ree to Lough Allen.
In the lake that you swim in your just tiny fry
Where everything gets on your nerves.
Down here you're the big fish that glides slowly by,
One who gets the respect he deserves.
The lassies down here are sure to beguile,
Oh sure it's a ball you'll be having,
And as for a strapping young lad with a smile,
You'll find them a-plenty in Cavan.
So come civil servants to Cavan to find,
Peace lapping on every lakeshore,
You'll blend with the natives so gentle and kind
And you never will leave us no more.

Giant Leabaigh's Rock

Some three miles west of Athlone, in the townsland of Meehanbee, in the parish of Drum, stands Giant Leabaigh's rock. That is what the locals called it. It is actually a huge dolmen. The great top stone that was meant to stand on six uprights is estimated to weigh twenty-four tons. However its great weight sunk some of the standing stones. As one end sunk the other end tilted up leaving two of the standing stones free of the top stone. The top stone now leans at a forty-five-degree angle.

Legendary "Piseóg's" superstition says that any interference with the monument will bring bad luck. The origin of this superstition is unclear but there are a number of possibilities. It may have carried down from very ancient times. However, just fifty yards from the rock we find a half made headstone with the name Reilly or Kelly engraved thereon. It appears that some stonemason, may have taken one of the uprights to fashion this stone and as he did not complete the job, he may have come to an untimely end. This could have started the superstition. Another remarkable thing about this dolmen is that it was lost to historians for hundreds of years. Perhaps people stopped talking about it after some unfortunate happening. It was only found to historians again about 1960, when this writer showed it to Billy English, a noted Athlone historian.

Local legend also has it that somewhere near this dolmen a poor farmer was digging in his field when the tip of his spade hit a rock. When he hit the rock again, three feet farther on he hoped it might be the same rock as long flat rocks were very useful for building chimneys. He was delighted to find that it was the same rock and after a lot of digging and scraping he found that the rock was ten feet long and ten feet wide and that the top of it was perfectly flat. Better still there was writing on it. Could it be a cover for buried treasure? Did the giant bury it?

He now had a dilemma, as he could not read. His wife could read but she was a gabby-gut who couldn't keep anything to herself and they were related to half the parish, all poor tenants like themselves who would expect to share in any good fortune. Then of course there was the landlord who, if he heard about it would just take the lot. He would have to trust the wife. Maybe if he brought her here he could keep her here until he lifted the stone and in that way she could not tell anyone. That night when they had their ten children put to bed he told her. "Come with me now" he said "and bring the lantern and we will see what the writing says."

The first line read in Gaelic, "Bfheidír go bhfuil an T-ádh leat?" "Perhaps the luck is with you?" The second line read, "Ardaigh suas mé agus feicfidh tu nios mó." "Raise me up and you will see more." This was very exciting information. They were sure it meant treasure. They would be rich. They would never again have to scrape and save and cow-tow to the landlord.

He decided to dig down beside the stone to find how thick it was. It was two feet thick. It would take several men to move it. They would have to share the treasure, but with whom? Just then their two oldest children arrived in their shimmies, Peig, thirteen and Padraig, twelve. The next six children followed them closely. The youngest two could not yet walk. Within a short time all ninety of the villagers had arrived. They all helped in the digging and soon they had the rock standing on its end. Two things became apparent; first, from a hole in the middle of the flat surface beneath the rock a little wisp of smoke emerged. Secondly, there was writing on the under side of the stone. In illuminated letters that were read out by the wife, "Lig anuas mé mar a bhí mé." "Put me down as I was before." There was silence for a few seconds before panic gripped the woman and she said, "On a count of three drop the rock." It fell with a great thud just as a wisp of smoke escaped at the side. Aaahhhh! Came a great unearthly blood-curling scream of pain as if somebody had their arm cut off. As the echoes from this scream died away terror gripped the crowd and all rushed to put the clay back on top of the rock with spades, shovels, sticks, feet or bare hands. Within ten minutes the clay was replaced so well that it looked exactly the same as the rest of the field. "Let no one ever speak of this night," said the oldest man in the village and they all slunk home petrified even to speak. Shortly after this the famine halved their number and those who survived never again mentioned "the" night. By the eighteen sixties people had again started to whisper about "the" night but by then nobody could agree exactly where the field was or even on whose land it was. As the field was thought to be cursed everybody said it was on other peoples land. However, it was definitely near Leabaigh's rock. About this time there was a long five-acre-field known as "The Gort Mór", "The Big Tillage Field". It was owned by Naghtens and leased in seven stripes to separate tenants. Maybe that was the field? Or maybe not? Or if it was on whose section was the stone? Now in 2006 the new motorway to Galway will be passing within a few hundred yards of Leabaigh's rock. If it runs through the field I wonder how the tree huggers will deal with an angry one-armed Genie? That is if it is his arm that is missing.

Some say that at certain times, in this area, you may even meet a wandering waving arm or fairy shimmering shimmied children or primitive ghostly diggers. Come if you dare to walk in their footsteps and see the Rock now that it is open to the public.

The Goose

Jim was dreaming that somebody was whinging about freezing feet and the hour of the night and somebody was drilling a hole in his head. Suddenly, he heard the screams. Jumping out of bed he ran down the stairs. He met Victoria, his wife.

"There's a dead bird in my new kitchen." Then he remembered he had won a live goose at the party last night. His newfound friend John had strangled it and left them both lying in the kitchen. He recovered and staggered up to bed. The goose didn't. John had also drunkenly told him how to pluck it, clean it and prepare it for the oven.

"Don't worry darling, I will pluck it and prepare it for cooking."

"Good," she said frostily.

"I am off to Dublin to collect my parents, the twins are still asleep, I will get breakfast on the road. I couldn't eat here now, I feel nauseous." Picking up the keys, she left.

As he was finishing the Alka-Seltzer, the twins appeared on the stairs.

"Where is Mama? We want our breakfast, we want fried bread sausages and Seven Up."

He gave them bread and jam and milk. This kept them quiet for a little while. He would work quickly and get the goose plucked before they finished.

Just three weeks ago, they had moved from Dublin 4 to this beautiful five-bedroom dormer on it's own grounds in Cavan. Victoria had designed the kitchen, with the electric cooker in the middle of the floor under a giant extractor fan. The cooker hob had a large flat surface area. He would do the plucking here. He placed the goose on the cooker, grabbed a bunch of feathers and pulled. Apart from hurting his hand, nothing happened. He would have to pull the feathers one at a time. By the time the twins had finished their breakfast he had extracted twenty-five feathers in an area of two square inches. He was surprised to find that the bloody bird had underwear, lovely and soft but impossible to remove. Then he remembered his old great-grandmother who had spent her last few months in their house when he and his brothers were children. Daft Granny they called her. She spoke a weird language and said silly things like,

"If you get up on an ass, you'll get down on a goose."

Now the penny dropped, even without getting up on the ass he had got the "down" on the goose. How the hell was he going to get the down off the goose?

"We will help," said the twins. Wasn't he lucky! Their third birthday was last week. All three were still in their pyjamas.

"Here pull the soft bits, a tiny bit at a time, Jack! Don't throw it at Denis, just put it down." The Alka-Seltzer wasn't working. He would have to get a hair of the dog, just a short to steady his hands. That helped and after a while the undressing was going well, more flesh was appearing and he and the twins were growing white beards and hair, "a bit like Santa," Denis said. The teddy bears on their slippers were also growing beards. The floor too, was turning white, the feathers and down was supposed to stay on the cooker top and not move around. Not to worry, he could easily tidy up afterwards. He hadn't noticed that the twins had gone upstairs to the toilet, to the guest room with grandpa's present, to their own room for the present, back again with grandma's present and to Mammy's room to roll in the lovely soft duvet and of course to see the Christmas tree in the sitting room. They had also got dressed, in a manner of speaking. He was still in his pyjamas and some goose clothing.

Now to move the naked bird to the sink for cleaning, oops! He had hit the switch on the extractor fan. Whoosh! It sucked up all the feathers, scrape! The fuses blew, with a sort of sneeze, it threw out all the feathers and down again over a wider area, over everything in the kitchen, the hall, the stairs and everywhere. Three year-olds do not close doors.

Leave that for now; get on with the cleaning the bird. How?

"Just put a cut at both ends and pull out the insides" that's what John said. That was easy but Oh! The smell. Was that the goose? No it was burning feathers, in the panic with the fan he had turned on one plate on the cooker. The feathers just crinkled up and turned black, some exploding on to the floor and walls, others caking on to the cooker. He rushed to switch it off, must be bloody voodoo. He didn't see the cat that had come with the house, coming in. Growling, the cat grabbed the entrails and made good his escape into the hall and upstairs leaving a feathery fence around his bloody trail. Victoria arrived with her parents, Alexandria and Ronald, the retired Judge. All four generations of Ronald's family had been members of the judiciary since his great grandfather came over as legal adviser to the Viceroy. Since then, they had never mingled with anybody from outside the Pale until Victoria had become infatuated with this Cork man. Glancing round the room he observed the devastation, the whiskey bottle and the glass with the feathers stuck to it. Ronald's worst fears were realised but he always knew the Irish man would revert to class and culture at the first opportunity. "Cavan was such an opportunity," and he had wasted no time, now he hoped his daughter would see sense and divorce him immediately.

Instead, having viewed the scene and seeing the little-boy-lost look on her Jimmy's face Victoria laughed heartily before melting into his feathery arms. The Judge and Alexandria threw arms and eyes heavenward before they too broke into laughter as he picked up the whiskey bottle and reached for fresh glasses from the cabinet. At last they had become Irish.

Mothers of the Celtic Tigers

It was just my luck to arrive in Carrignaros on pig fair day. The entire main street was full of tractors and trailers and a few horse carts full of pigs. This was a normal small town setting in nineteen seventy-four. I had to park my car two hundred yards from the hotel where I had a lunch appointment and walk through the fair. Luckily I was used to farm situations so I was not nauseated by the smell.

As I picked my steps through the throng, I noticed two tractor-trailers backed up to a dealer's lorry. There was a litter of finished pigs in each trailer, ten in one and eleven in the other. I was well aware that it took considerable skill and dedicated husbandry to bring those numbers to maturity. At the time the average litter would have been about eight. The floor of the lorry was three feet higher than the trailer's. Two men of advancing years were endeavouring, with little success, to lift the first of the fifteen-stone pigs onto the lorry.

Just then two red-haired women hopped up on the trailer, said, "stand back men," and took over the loading. They both grabbed a front leg below the knee and a back leg above the knee and before the pig knew what hit him, he had been thrown into the lorry. These were fine well built, well-padded, elegant women, perhaps early forties. They were evidently sisters and appeared to be spouses of the two much older men. No doubt they had married them in the depressed fifties when they were strong farmers financially, though physically past their peak. As they continued the work a small crowd gathered to admire.

I proceeded to my appointment while surmising their situation. Those animals had probably been brought to maturity with produce laboriously grafted from the stony grew soil of Monaghan. A lucky sow treated with tender loving care could produce two litters a year. It would supplement the children's allowance, the turkey money and other farm income. Even an aging man could manage a farm, operate a tractor, buy and sell things and keep a woman company, no use letting him strain his heart.

Just as we were finishing our lunch in the pub, the two men came in, followed a little way behind by the women. As he reached the bar one of the men turned and said,

"Well women, what will ye have?" The reply came in unison,

"Whiskey."

This Emigrant Remembers

This emigrant remembers, though a long way have I come,
Through miles and years and places, from my home in dear old Drum.
We went to school barefooted and we played the "CLUICHE PEIL"
And with homemade ash "COMÁNS" we hit the "SLIOTAR" true and well.

And the smoke curled ever skywards, in dreams I see it still,
When the "droppeen" of the "CHREATURE" was distilled on Glanmore hill.
We rowed along the Shannon with the young lads from Clonown
And we left them all behind us, at the boat race in the town.

We cut the turf in Gorry in the heather scented air
Serenaded by the skylark, 't was a little heaven there.
And we danced in good old Kielty, at the Maypole and in Moore.
Sure the craic and sport was mighty, we didn't know that we were poor.

Then the days were long and sunny and the flowers were all in bloom
And we courted half the night, the lovely maidens in Kiltoom.
But the wanderlust was on me, but I did mean to come back,
When I'd gather up the money in Aussieland's outback.

The day I sheared three hundred sheep Paddy put the rest to shame
And I scoffed at lesser Shearer's and basked in the acclaim.
The day I heard my loved one died, the shock and shiver's with me yet,
And I prayed and cursed and cried and got drunk just to forget.

So I sheared their smelly sheep amid the grime and sweat and tears
And drank gallons of their whiskey and didn't mind the passing years.
But when my strength began to fail and liver felt all-queer
They put me rolling fleeces, for I could no longer shear.

So I took my little pension and across the world I've come,
To visit my relations, in Clonown, Kiltoom and Drum.
But the young gaze blank upon me, as they sit and drink in bars,
Or blow me off the road, as they flit about in cars.

"Oh where are my lovely friends? They're all old or dead and gone,
Is this where it all ends? Is it time that I passed on?
May the great Lord look upon me, may he let me know the truth?
Am I pining for old Ireland? Or just my long lost youth?"

Hearseless Funeral from Drumlosh 1943

As I recall, the house was the last one on the road, with only a field running down to the Shannon. The funeral was similar to any other, with mourners all around as the coffin rested on four chairs outside the front door, prior to being shouldered by four male namesakes. As they moved onto the road, "Oh horror!"... There was no hearse. Not to worry, they turned toward the open field leading down to the Shannon. Having escaped the boundary walls of the road, the cortege fanned out bringing all the mourners into a large circle as they crossed the soft ground to the water's edge. There was a sort of eerie silence as their feet made no sound on the grass.

Crouching boatmen held two cots and a rowboat alongside the bank. Cots were very large heavy rowboats used for funerals, special occasions and ferrying hay off islands on the river. The first cot had two planks placed across it amidships. With considerable skilled manoeuvring the coffin was placed on the planks while the mourners poured shakily into all three boats. As there was not room for all, many women, children and old people stayed on the bank. As a strong breeze blew up the river from the south, conditions were choppy and dangerous for the overloaded boats. As the boats moved out to the deep, at an angle into the wind, the water was almost lapping over the edge. A child called out, "Oh the woman in the coffin will be drowned!" "She is the only safe one afloat!" replied an old man.

No mishap occurred and the old woman was interred in Saint Kieran's Holy Ground, "Seven Churches" from whence 'tis said God calls to himself nine out of ten, while in other areas the proportion is much less.

Go nDeanfaidh Dia trocaire ar a anam.

God rest her soul.

The Corncrake

When we were young in the nineteen fifties we used to discuss what the birds said. We could never agree about the black bird, the thrush or indeed any other songbird but we all knew what the corncrake said. He went "grake grake, grake grake, grake grake" and everybody knew that meant, stand back, stand back, stand back. At that time there was a corncrake in every field in Ireland.

At this time there was a certain young girl who had just turned sixteen, and she had her mother annoyed to let her go to a dance in the town, but there was no way her mother would agree as she did not have a chaperone and towns fellows were not to be trusted. Then luck struck. The local GAA club hired a big tent in which to run a carnival for two weeks and it was close by the girl's house. Now she could go dancing.

She cycled to town and bought a lovely piece of material and a pattern. The material was spread out on the kitchen table, the pattern carefully spread on top. There was great excitement. The mother was more jittery than the daughter. They had just got in the electricity. They had a brand new singer sewing machine. "We will put in shoulder pads and you can wear your new bra. I will lend you my black patent belt to match the shoes, sure it would go twice round your little waist." These were modern times. For the moment meals were suspended. The men could grumble and wait. Oh it was wonderful, Harry Belafonte was singing on the wireless,

"I see woman on bended knee, cutting cane for her family,"

"Well God be with the days."

"I see man by the waterside, casting nets at the surging tide."

"He might as well be, as looking for a bit to eat round here." In spite of those unhelpful remarks and a few miner glitches the needlework classes paid off, the project was successful and the dress was completed. Now for the hair! All hell broke loose.

After tea, her mother rolled her hair on her finger and held each curl in place with a pipe cleaner. It took ages and was sometimes painful but there were no complaints. You have to suffer to be beautiful. Next day, when the pipe cleaners were removed the hair brushed out perfectly. On the night when she put on the multi coloured dress over the new bra, with the shoulder pads and the patent belt, she was beautiful. Even the hungry grumblers agreed.

"Mammy" she said,

"What is it a Gra?" (Love)

"If a boy wants to walk me home after the dance, will it be alright?"

"I suppose as the place is well lit up and if he is a nice respectable country boy, it will."

"Mammy."

"What is it now child?"

"If the boy wants to kiss me will I let him?"

The mother thought for a moment, her mind was racing, racing back to her own youth, her dreams, her dilemmas, her desires,

"You can if you both agree to obey the corncrake and when he calls stand back, you're to stand back."

As it happened the boy who walked her home on the night, was a friend of mine and next morning I waylaid him.

"Well how did you get on?"

"How did I get on?" says he, with some agitation.

"I'll tell you how I got on! You know as well as I know that the sweet girl lives only a hundred yards from the marquee, and I walked her home all of five miles but we never did get away from the blooming corncrake."

The Game of Pitch and Toss

Head's a tanner, head's a tanner, that's what might be heard from a "gossen" on a misty Sunday evening on the Bridle Road in the nineteen forties or fifties. That's where the game of pitch and toss took place. A tanner was a sixpenny bit with a greyhound on it and it could buy you ten woodbines or gain you admission to the Maypole – an open air dance held on slabs of maple floor with the band playing in a sort of covered tree house. So it was a brave "gossen" who would risk that much on one toss, brave or foolish or nearly a man. Then again he might be a regular who knew the tosser was a man who could head boot nails and felt he could fool some teenager on their first night out. Those were decadent days. This was illegal activity but I never heard of anybody being prosecuted for it. In any case we would see the Clonark guards coming at Hukies and we would have plenty of time to pick up the money. To play pitch and toss you first put a stone the size of a tennis ball on the road and took five paces back and drew a line on the road with your boot. The stone was called a "Bob". All pitchers had to toe this line when pitching. The first pitcher pitched two pennies as near the "Bob" as possible. The penny nearest the bob counted as his pitch while the second pitcher picked up the penny farthest from the "Bob" and this penny became known as the "rout". At this stage the first pitcher usually announced, "the rout is mine." The second pitcher then pitched the rout, followed by a penny of his own. Again only the penny nearest the bob counted and the rout was picked up and used in the same way by the third pitcher and so on with each other pitcher. When every player had pitched the owner of the penny nearest the Bob took over the tossing. If the distance from the Bob seemed similar for two pennies a blade of grass was used to measure the difference.

The tosser then picked up all the pennies, gave the rout back to its owner and put the rest in his pocket. The word tosser denoted the man or nearly a man, tossing the pennies but a single penny was also called a tosser as in "I haven't a tosser." No women ever played, as it was strictly "a man's game". To confuse matters further the comb or piece of timber upon which the pennies were placed for tossing was also called the tosser. The tosser then took a comb or a piece of wood the shape of a comb out of his breast pocket and put two pennies on it with the harps facing up. Some times those pennies would be from the pitched pennies but the more experienced players would have special tossing pennies, which they always used and which were kept in a special pocket. At this stage, while holding the pennies in place with his thumb the tosser threw a shilling or two shilling piece or even a half a crown on the ground and said "cover that." The other players between them then threw down enough money to cover what he had thrown, some sixpence, some three pence, some a shilling and so on. Then there would be some side betting between outsiders, hence the call "heads a tanner" inviting a bet.

Finally the two pennies were thrown up in the air to calls of "give them sky." This was to insure fair toss and also to intimidate the tosser. If the pennies came down two heads, the tosser won, if two harps, the other people won, or if one head and one harp he had to toss them again and keep doing so until he got a result. He had four tosses in all so if he won the first he just picked up his original wager and the losers covered it again. After he had his four tosses, those which were headed, were deemed spent but any tosses harped went to the pitcher who was second. If he had any tosses harped they went to the pitcher who was third and so on. During all this there would be calls of two heads or two harps or head harp intermingled, with an occasional profanity. This was when a tourist visiting Ireland wrote about a holy nation where large groups of men spent hours on Sundays looking up to sky and down to the ground while loudly invoking the Holy Name. Were we all heavenly bound?

As you can see, it was always necessary to have four times your first bet as you might lose all four tosses. Many a young fellow lost his first weeks wages here and it was generally agreed that it was cheap education, as once bitten twice shy. Then some kept lucky pennies just for tossing, sometimes healthy Irish pennies with the hen and her clutch of lucky chickens or old English pennies with the King's head on one side and the Devil with the three-pronged fork on the other. The latter were favoured by older men as they learned their trade before the Irish money came in. There was considerable skill in tossing as proven by the experienced winners. The stance, the flick of the wrist, the way you held your mouth, the weather, the softness of the ground, were all contributing factors to the way the pennies fell. At that time most men wore nail boots and of course everybody knew that if boot nails were thrown in the air they would always fall heads down, hence the saying "he could head boot nails."

Occasionally and particularly after a "gossen" had won a tanner or two there might be a flare up and the "gossen" might be attacked physically or verbally and a call made for all "gossens" to go home and learn their books. This called for a discreet but temporary retreat by the youngsters. In any case we all knew that you could cover a half crown with sixty halfpennies, thirty pennies, ten three-penny bits, six tanners, a two-shilling piece and a tanner, two single shillings and a sixpence or any combination of the above. We also knew that there were four hundred and eighty half-pence or two hundred and forty pennies in a pound and that there was half that in a ten bob note, one eighth of it in a half-crown, one-tenth of it in a florin, one-twentieth in a shilling, one-fortieth in a tanner and one-eightieth in a three-penny bit. We had a good grounding in one of the three R's and in all three of the Ds, "devilment, daring and deviousness."

The proximity of the gamble to the Maypole created still more problems for young players as the lure of the music, the thought of the dancers and the desire for female company could interfere with concentration and leave a "man" without the admission money not to mention sweets for a girl or fags for the week. Every dance that was called, was yet another chance for non-gamblers to chat up the girls, yet a fellow would surely hit pay dirt with the next toss. Decisions, decisions or indeed indecision would probably see him lose out on both counts. Or was it the dirty hands that did him?

Beginners often started by pitching only, as this could be done with just one-penny capital. If he won the pitch he would first pocket all the pennies and then sell the toss to some experienced person. In this way a "gossen" could acquire some gambling capital and an addiction from which he might never recover. Then again you must play the hand you are dealt. The penny for this start might often be found at the scene of the gamble the morning after as the game usually went on until almost complete darkness. God switched off the light.

We heard that there were gambles in Drum, Clonark, Kiltoom and out the far side of the town and we assumed they were country-wide. Yet we felt that ours was the only honest one and that it might be dangerous to play anywhere else. Didn't we know everyone here and they were all decent people. No, no, no, there could be nothing wrong with our hobby. Despite exhortations from mothers, wives, priests and parsons, nothing, but nothing, neither loss of heaven or fear of hell could cure our addiction. Until television arrived.

Bricks on the Hob

Old Jenny was a teacher of Maths, that real hard job,
Old Sonny was the painter of bricks upon the hob,
And as he did the painting he explained it all so good,
And she, his words corrected, because she felt she should.

At first he did the arch, with every leaning brick,
And fitted in the co-op stone, while saying that's the trick
It's not co-op, it's coping, that's what she said, said she,
Co-op or cope what matter, they're all the same said he.

The three cornered brick to level, he said was five four three,
The long side is high pothooks, it fits like that you see.
Hypotenuse the long side, that's what she said, said she,
Hypotenuse, high pothooks, they're all the same said he.

And as he did the painting, now watch this close said he,
For with the old thick neck of it, you'll also paint like me.
The word it is technique, that's what she said, said she,
Technique, thick neck what matter? They're all the same said he.

The Moon

Ah! God be with the days when people actually looked at the moon, talked about the moon, dreamed about the moon, sometimes even talked to the moon or the man thereon. I see the moon the moon sees me, that's where my heart is longing to be. That's what the hit song said. Do lovers today ever look at the moon? If they do they keep it to themselves. They never sing about it, sigh about it or talk to it. I don't believe they even know it's there. It's all Neil Armstrong's fault, if he had only kept his big dirty boots off it, things might be different.

Before sex or television came to Ireland the moon was very important. What else was there for secretive young lovers to watch or talk about? All young love was secretive then. To have the pale silvery light of the moon shining on a loved ones face was the stuff of dreams, of songs of longing, loving and leaving to toil in foreign parts. Those were romantic times when love was always unrequited, when parting was the norm and kissing goodbye was the ultimate in satisfaction. Those were the days when all love songs were poignantly and beautifully sad, with a promise of better times to come.

When travel was difficult or impossible, there were no phones, faxes, texting or emailing, one could look at the moon and know that the distant lover was looking at the same moon. One could even talk to the moon and send messages of love far deeper in desire and execution than might be possible at close quarters. One could even imagine the loved one doing the same thing. Of course the loved one could be sending gushing passionate messages of love via the moon to somebody else. It doesn't bear thinking about. Then again the moon probably would not pass on the messages, so there might be no harm done. The moon is always unreliable; it has nothing definite, no clear light, no date and it's always coming and going. You could say that something happened in a particular month like September or March or you could have definite years like 1955 or 2005. But whoever heard of moon number 3897 or 9873 or any other number for that matter. Even when it's there, it's seldom all there and when it's gone it's never heard of again. Wouldn't all this just make you want to howl at the moon?

A new moon, like new love is a sliver, develops into a waxing crescent then on to the first quarter that is really a half. From there it soon reaches a waxing gibbons and in another few days, a full moon. If it's not the real thing, from here it's all down hill, from full moon to waning gibbons to last quarter and lastly to waning crescent, sad, final and finished, never to be seen again nor even remembered. When the moon is gone, while sweet memories may linger, that moon is forgotten forever.

Old wives had "piseóg's" superstitions about things that occurred during different phases of the moon and indeed about the different shapes of the moon. I never heard of anything that old husbands said but I suppose that's because they didn't have any say. Some things never change.

It was always best if you met a potential soul mate in the first quarter of the moon. The way the waxing crescent is lying is most important. If he is lying on his back he is drunk, unpredictable and happy, the life and soul of the party, one who will sweep you off your feet, promise you the world, make you feel the most important and most loved person ever, ruffle your heart and do the same thing for your best friend.

If the new crescent stands erect your chosen one will be hard working, careful, straight-laced reliable, trustworthy and may bore you to death. On the other hand, whatever takes your fancy.

If your new crescent is leaning slightly you may be looking good. He may have all the charms of the first mentioned with none of the problems. He also may have all the advantages of number two without any of the boring traits. If those two things occur simultaneously you may be on a winner but beware the leaning crescent that may have the bad points of everybody and the good points of none. If you have been listening carefully you should now be an expert on the first phase of love, in the first quarter of the moon and what pitfalls may be encountered. Of course if you have not interpreted those words properly your assessments may be erroneous.

Even if you have you must now follow up on the further development of the moon until it is full. Among the things to consider here are the number and times of meetings; are they all by moonlight? Is the moon sometimes clouded over? Does it cloud over during the meeting? If the clouds are scudding across the moon, does your dear one look more appealing at every brightening or do they look or feel better in the dark? There might be a hint of things to come here. Then again there might not. What do you think? What should you think? What does your head say? What does your heart say? What is the other half thinking? Now that the moon is full are either of you mad? Madly in love or madly out of love or just plain mad? Will it grow deeper or will it wane with the waning moon and disappear on the 28th day? Perhaps it's time to go in out of the cold, without the white heat of passion, you might catch a chill, or worse still your lover might be the one lacking passion. One never knows what "two does."

Whispers

Having just qualified as a national teacher, Jimmy applied for a number of jobs, permanent and temporary. In the nineteen thirties jobs were scarce and all he got was a temporary post in a two-teacher country school. The Master, who was also the principal, had got a heart attack. The aging female assistant taught the infant classes so he took third, fourth, fifth and sixth classes (8 to 12 year olds). The mixed school worried him a bit as he had only ever attended all boys schools.

The management board, which consisted of the old Parish Priest, assured him that good digs had been booked for him adjacent to the school. On the Sunday evening, having taken himself, his luggage and his bicycle off the Dublin train at Athlone, he cycled the ten miles to Coolmore parochial house that was beside the school.

"Just a mile up the byroad there," the Parish Priest said after he showed him the school. The Widow Malone's house is the one with the slated room. The poor woman's husband died last year and she needs the money and of course she has the slated room. At that time whenever a legacy came from America, people who lived in thatched houses would build a two-storey slated room on to the end of the house.

Having cycled for a few miles he arrived for the evening meal. The widow, a buxom woman in her forties introduced him to her seven daughters, all striking redheads ranging in ages from nine to nineteen. Starting with the youngest she gave their names as, Mary, Third Class, Meabh, Fourth Class, Mena, Fifth Class, Maureen, Sixth Class, Nance, Delia and Lorna who worked in the local bar and grocery. She had auburn hair, huge brown eyes and the most dazzling smile he had ever seen.

Where were they all going to sleep? Not to worry, upstairs in the slated room was his bedroom. It was en suite, that is, it had a wooden washstand, complete with basin, ewer (large jug) full of water and waste bucket. The privy was out behind the cowshed. As well as underwear she would wash three shirts and seven collars weekly for him. Shirt collars were held on with studs in those days. Jimmy had grown up in Dublin with all modern conveniences, electricity, running water and proper bathroom. He and his younger brother had their own rooms. He had been thrown in at the deep end a week before his twenty-first birthday.

School went grand, even though he taught four children with whom he lived. As they sat down for the evening meal, Mary announced that the turkey was "lying". From the glances that ran round the table he felt he should say something.

"Is she sick?" Peels of laughter followed. He felt his face redden.

"Stud" said Delia from under the laughter.

"Did she swallow a stud?"

This time the laughter went totally out of control.

"Is that how they do it in Dublin?" followed by more laughter.

"Leave the poor man alone," said the widow.

"He's from Dublin and doesn't understand those things."

At this time every rural village had a strong farmer's wife who held a turkey cock at stud.

Noticing his extreme embarrassment, Lorna tried to smother the laughter. For five years now she had been ogled by beer swilling, bar stool boors, none of whom enhanced her view of men. Now she had her very own tall, tame, tanned, teetotal teacher living in her house, she was not about to let him escape. She was sure she would have the support of her mother and sisters, except perhaps, Nance and Delia who might fancy their own chances. She would ask her mother's advice.

"Take him to the whispering arch at Seven Churches," her mother said but "Don't tell him anything about it, just start a little whispering and take it from there." Seven Churches was the local name for Clonmacnoise.

In the fifteenth century Dean Odo Malone of Clonmacnoise commissioned a great sculptor to carve and fit a new stone door surround on the north side of the cathedral. Into this surround he cut several half pipes going right over the top and down both sides. If words are whispered into one of those half pipes on one side, a listener with an ear to the other side can pick up the whisper clearly. However a voice will not carry in the pipes. The speaker has to face the wall but the listener has a rear view of the whisperer. A conversation between a young couple was much more romantic when whispered through ancient stone pipes, even if one party didn't really know that the chat was meant to be romantic in the first place.

They would cycle there after school. He always wanted to visit Saint Kieran's holy city. The ruins of the cathedral that was burned down by the English hundreds of years ago stand in the middle of a walled graveyard. There are the various superstitions that have grown since. That's why the mother advised the special visit.

When he had climbed the four steps to the top of the stile he turned and took her outstretched hand to help her up. As there was very little space on the top step and she was afraid of heights he had to hold on to her as he helped her down. She giggled and he blushed. As the ground was uneven across the graves, they had to hold hands for balance. There was nobody about only old Mary Martin down in the new graveyard tending her husband's grave. By the time they reached the doorway Lorna thought she had a midge in her eye. While bending over her upturned face he thought he removed it with his handkerchief. Again she giggled and again he blushed.

Jimmy was enthralled by the complete round tower and even more so by the incomplete round tower.

"Why is it incomplete?" he asked.

"Put your ear to the wall and you'll hear what happened."

When he did he heard her whispered reply,

"A lovers tiff; when his lover jilted him for the builder he climbed up and started knocking the tower. All efforts to stop him failed until the lover promised to come back to him but then the builder refused to repair the damage and so it remains to this day."

"Is this true?"

"Many people round Seven Churches think so."

"Do you believe it?"

"It's a good romantic story and I love romance."

"Have you much experience?"

"Very little, where would it come from in a place like this, but sure we live in hope, what about you?"

"Totally lacking experience but now that I'm working I might make up for lost time." Every time he turned his head to listen and watch, she became more desirable. Little did he know that her mind was made up since Sunday evening when first she set eyes on him. Then again, hadn't he been completely bowled over by her beauty from the start.

That was how their conversation continued over the next half hour, each whispering their piece to the wall then watching the back of the others head while listening to the reply. They didn't notice old Mary approaching from behind.

"It's grand to see young lovers using the arch," she said,

"Fifty seven years ago my Paddy whispered his proposal and I whispered my yes. Fifty seven years of love and contentment we've had, thank you Dean Odo," she said looking up at the arch.

"How long is he dead now?"

"He went with the daffodils, he's making a straw súgán chair for me in heaven, he'll have it ready for me for Christmas." She then turned to Jimmy, placed a bony hand on his arm and with the slanting September sun from Connaught shining on her face, she looked him straight in the eye and said, "This is the most important day in your life, don't let it slip away." This time they both blushed. After she left Jimmy found himself saying to the stone, "Give me a kiss?" as he turned to seek reaction instead of answering she was smiling up at him in gorgeous, glowing, glorious anticipation.

Before she rounded the corner of the cathedral, old Mary looked back at the embracing couple, smiled a wrinkly smile, turned and shuffled off toward heaven.

Woollen Mills Fire

When I awoke in the middle of the night, the light was jumping on the walls. I jumped out of bed. Mammy was missing from her bed. I ran down to the kitchen where I met Delia who had come back for me.

"The war has started," she said.

"And the town is on fire. Put on your boots and coat and come out to look." I got dressed and we were on our way in an instant. The rest of the family were all up on the hill looking at the fire in town. That's the lights I saw jumping on the walls.

"Bring the child here to me," Mammy said, as she put her arm round me. The seven of us were all close together, watching and praying for the people in the town.

"The aeroplanes must be very high up as we cannot hear them," Mammy said.

"But I suppose they're gone now that the damage is done." After a while, Peter came back from Lennon's shop where he had gone for news of how things were in town.

"It's not the Germans at all," he said,

"It's the woollen mills that's on fire and they say it will burn the whole town."

"Have they no way to quench it?"

"Only buckets of water from the river Shannon. The army is helping the town's people but they haven't got enough buckets. They're using every vessel in the town."

"See there, the fire is the far side of the new church." We could see that he was right.

"Thanks be to God it's not the war," Mammy said. Just then we heard the bombs.

"Oh glory be to God, it is the war, don't you hear the bombs, why can't we see the aeroplanes? They must be too high up; you couldn't be up to the Germans. What will happen now? Will there be conscription? They will have to leave some men to work the land. Sure Germany will overrun the country in a few days anyway. What will happen then?"

"The man on the bike that cycled from town must be mistaken" said Peter.

"I suppose they bombed the woollen mills because they were sending woollens to England for the army. What will we do with the wool now?

"It's a wonder they didn't bomb the new church," said Mammy.

"No they're keeping that as a marker for the army barracks."

"Why didn't they bomb the barracks now?"

"Maybe they think the Irish army will join them against England."

"They wouldn't, would they?"

"You'd never know; it might be the safest thing to do. Germany ran through Poland and the other countries without any bother. It's not two years yet since the war started and they're here, it's probably no use fighting them. We have no tanks or aeroplanes. I'll go back to Lennon's to see if there is more news."

When he was gone we started the rosary. Although there were no more bombs the fire burned as bright as ever with the flames going as high at the twin steeples of the new church. After a long time Peter returned with the news that it was not the Germans at all, only a fire in the woollen mills.

"But we heard the bombs," said Mammy.

"The Irish army had to blow up all the buildings round the mill in order to stop the fire. Luckily nobody was killed or injured. Everybody in the town is in there now throwing water on the rubble to stop the fire."

"Thank God it's not the war but with the mills gone, where will all the people work?"

"If they go to England they will have to go to the war or down the mines."

"Sure they might build the mills again."

"That will take years. What will they do in the meantime?"

" I suppose some might get jobs building it."

"We can only pray for them." This we did as the fire continued and then went back to bed.

To My Mother

Your courage was amazing
As you faced the war alone
For the economic thirties
Had claimed your spouse and first born son.

You held us as all together
Praying for the burning town,
For you thought the war had landed
The night the woollen mills burned down.

As we walked to Mass together
In the darkness of the morn`
You gently rubbed our hands and ears,
To keep the circulation going.

For years you struggled in the hayfields
And the rains were coming down
And you faced midlife alone
With no mate to help you on.

When teenage stamina came to me
Coursed through muscle, voice and vein,
With pride I took your hayfork
Farm work you'd never do again.

You're long with my Dad in heaven
Your brood arriving one by one
And I know some day I'll join you
When like you my work is done.

The Curse of the Ritz

Now that the majestic new building has arisen phoenix like, in Custume Place, spare a thought for the once glamorous Ritz cinema and its legendary curse.

It all started the evening that the cement check showed five bags over. At that time cement arrived by train to Athlone's Southern Station, from where Lister's men brought it by horse and cart to their premises in Pearse Street, a ton at a time. As the site of the Ritz was on the way, they delivered direct from the wagon but they only brought fifteen hundred weight at a time, as the hill down by Liptons was very steep and the horses would not be able to hold back a ton. If the britchel was to break, the whole lot might end up in the Shannon. The britchel was the braking system on the horse and cart. Occasionally a bag of cement might go missing, or once, when somebody forgot to cover a couple of bags the night before and they were rock solid in the morning, they were quickly consigned to the deep before the foreman saw them.

Even after a major inquiry among carters, clerks, railway men, tradesmen, labourers and foremen, nobody could explain where five extra bags of cement came from, but rumours abounded, one of which was that an under strength mix was put in one of the pillars supporting the structure. When an enthusiastic young missioner visiting the new Saint Peters Church called all cinemas dens of iniquity, a cantankerous old lady who wholeheartedly agreed with him foretold that the suspect pillar would collapse some night of a full house, and all the sinners would be drowned in the good Irish Shannon. Not one would be saved, from the grandees in the half crown gallery to the fourpenny pits. That they say is how the rumour started but as time passed, everybody heard it but few heeded it.

About this time there was a friar whom we will call "Friar Justin" stationed in Athlone. He had a certain reputation as a confessor. Let's say, only old ladies and strangers used his confessional while large crowds queued outside the other five boxes. When an occasional teenager from an outlying parish like Brideswell or Ballinahown or Tang felt that his sins had become too big for his own parish, there was nothing for it but to get on his bicycle and hit for the Friary. On arrival he found five confessionals with large queues and one with nobody at all. He took the course of least resistance, which perhaps was the character trait, which got him here in the first place. Almost immediately a tirade erupted from the confessional, sometimes overflowing into the church. Eventually it died down and the penitent emerged from Friar Justin, cleansed, chastised and chastened, only to have to run the gauntlet of a "sneer" of sniggering smart "alecs" muttering snide asides about "who's the girl?" He was horrified, humiliated and heartbroken that the angelic object of his affections should be defiled in all her soft sweet sinfulness, in the sewer mouths and minds of those blasphemous, bombastic buffoons or as he muttered to himself, "bad bloody bastards." By now, his own Parish Priest seemed just a pussycat.

The aforementioned Friar Justin had a great love of films or the pictures, as they were then known, however as one who had taken a vow of poverty, he could only attend on invitation. The manager of the Ritz was a prudent and pragmatic man who fancied an each way insurance bet and he was kind enough to offer the Friar a free seat for every opening night. These occurred at least once and sometimes two or three times a week and the Friar always attended. He never knew that his special seat was the one directly over the suspect pillar. Well the ruse worked. Whether by divine intervention or otherwise, the Ritz stood proud to the end for all of sixty years. Many if not most of the characters mentioned have gone to their eternal reward. We remember them with great affection: may they rest in peace.

Shy Man

Even though he was seven years her senior, Paddy had been admiring Mary from a distance for many years. Not that it did him any good because he lacked the courage to do anything about it. Oh he had plenty of courage on the football field or handling livestock but with girls it was different. He often started out determined to carry through but always chickened out at the last minute. Whenever he practised a few sentences in front of the mirror they sounded great but he could never repeat the words when faced with Mary, her half smile, her feminine gait, her air of serenity. Her gentleness just melted his heart and tied his tongue. With a mumbled hello his jellied legs always scuttled him away.

Now it was different, his Mother had died six long months ago last spring, the loneliness was unbearable, Mary was always on his mind and he would turn forty before Christmas. He just had to kick himself into action. He thought of a plan. Mary lived with her brother Tom who played cards in the village every Tuesday night.

At that time the carbide lamp was the latest status symbol of dashing young men. It was a sophisticated piece of equipment. It had a bottom chamber for white carbide powder, a higher chamber with water that dripped on to the powder, forming a flammable gas, a jet protruding into the light chamber where the gas would be lit by a match and finally a little glass door to protect the flame. There was a screw tap to accurately control the water flow as too little or too much yielded no gas. There was also a built-in pump to keep the gas pressed through the jet at the right speed to create a perfect blue flame. The mirror type reflector then threw the light onto the road ahead when the whole contraption was clipped on to the bicycle. In the event of power failure, it would be necessary to call to the nearest house for light to reset the whole thing.

Now for the plan. He would call to Mary's house on Tuesday night to regulate his carbide lamp. He would call with the lamp in his hand, then even if his voice failed him, she would know what he wanted and she would invite him into the light. Then as he dazzled her with his dexterity, technical wizardry and ultra-modern equipment, speech would surely come. She might even offer him tea. He would look at her, admire her, and just be beside her. She would smile at him; oh that smile! No, no this was too good to be true. Something would go wrong. Don't be negative, what can go wrong? There will be only the two of us and after a while his courage would come.

He knocked at the door. Mary opened it. He held up the lamp.

"Paddy; you want to regulate your lamp, come into the light, Lorna's girls are here visiting. They came to say goodbye, Meg and Peg are for America tomorrow." The kitchen was full of big redhead girls, four of them, all late teens. They were nieces; her older sister Lorna had married Big Red Hanrahan from the mountain over twenty years ago. They had wild sons who emigrated but not before they had made a name for themselves fighting at football matches and dances. He hoped the girls would be more agreeable. They weren't.

"Did your little blue light go out?" Loud laughter,

"Was it ever lit?" More laughter,

"Is your carbide dry?"

"No his pump is faulty,"

"I think it's his little jet," hysterical laughter. They had certainly taken after their father, loud brash manner, roaring red hair, big noses and little beady eyes. Mary had disappeared.

He ran from the house, clasping his lamp, a broken man, distraught, humiliated, broken-hearted with the salt tears of anger, frustration and failure burning his eyes, the coarse, squealing, mocking laughter ringing in his ears. Talk about bold, bawdy, brazen lady-dogs, those were they. Nothing could go wrong, like always, nothing went right. He had really blown all his chances with Mary now. He would never live it down. He would have to emigrate. He would have to live his whole life without love or companionship, without Mary. The thought was unbearable. He was definitely a case for the foreign legion, without hope.

When he reached his bike, Mary was there. She left her hand on his and smiling said, yes is my answer to your question. They needed no light after that.

The Pope in Galway

When grey dawn broke one misty morn
O'er Galway's race course wide
Then youth emerged from sleeping bags
Like newborn butterflies.

Their vigil kept throughout the night,
In bag or bus or car,
They came from homes throughout Ireland,
The youth from near and far.

Then screaming through the morning air
Came helicopters loud
And John Paul was standing there
Hands raised in blessing crowd.

His words came in compassion wrapped,
In loving phrases bound
And in those words, inspired and true,
Was deep faith to be found?

He gave them guides by which to live,
In most harmonious way,
He told the youth that he loved them
And trusted them that day.

And Godly vibes with saintly hue,
Went flowing o'er the crowd,
With wild, restrained, effusion,
They sang heart deep and loud.

Famed bishops and great singing priests,
Seemed merely atoms then
For God had sent his vicar here
To stir the hearts of men.

And though it be a thousand years
Before he comes again,
His loving words and smiling tears
Will guard our faith 'till then.

Sweetest Words

Minding the cows in the callow all day was not too hard but the fear of the German bombers was the problem. You never knew when they might come and you might not have time to hide. I decided to build an air raid shelter just big enough to hold one small boy. I flattened out a roadway, a foot wide in a big clump of rushes and then I tied the tops of the remaining rushes on both sides of the road making a little tunnel into which I could crawl whenever I heard an aeroplane. If they could not see me they could not bomb me.

The problem was that the ten-acre callow was long and narrow running from the road to the river. The big clumps of rushes were half way down and my job was to keep the cattle from going the road whenever the warble fly attacked. The warble fly only attacked when the sun was shining so that on a fine day he could attack any time, whereas on a cloudy day he did not appear at all. On showery days he always attacked when the sun reappeared so you could see it coming.

The warble fly is a very smart fellow while the cows are stupid. You see the warble fly must use his stinger to inject his eggs into the cow's hind quarters. The cow has a tail just in the right place to swot the fly as he carries out this painful task, painful for the cow that is. In order to avoid the tail the warble fly signals his intent to attack with a loud buzz,

"I'm going to sting, I'm going to sting, I'm going to sting," and the stupid cow puts her tail high on her back and runs aimlessly for her life. Then the fly zooms in and injects his eggs just where the tail should have been. Even if the cow reacts then and swats the fly it's no use as the evil deed is done and the eggs will live inside the cow's skin until next year. That's why a small boy had to spend his days keeping the foolish cows in their field. Old James said that God created the warble fly to make young calves run and make their lungs strong against pneumonia but people said he was doting.

Every morning I brought the dog Bruno with me for company but every day the mammy hare came limping on three legs and the fool of a dog chased her, she always went by a circuitous route the half mile to our house and then speeded up whereupon the dog gave up the chase, forgot about me and stayed at home all day. I tried playing with a field mouse instead. I was trying to catch him for days but one day I got to pin him under some rushes. When I had him pinned I could see his back but I wanted to get a better look. I decided to catch him by the end of his tail so I could have a good look while he dangled upside-down. In a flash he curled up on his tail and bit my index finger peeling a white drill from the middle joint to the nail. In fright and pain I released him as I saw the white teeth track turn to blood, two slice cuts with a drill in the middle where his teeth were spaced. Of course I failed to stamp on him and he escaped. I would be smarter next time.

The very next day I had him pinned under the rushes again. I caught him very tight by the back of the neck and held him up in front of my face. It was a mammy mouse with two rows of freshly sucked tits running down her belly. As I looked into her frightened eyes, her whiskered nose and her little parted teeth, I said "I have you now and there is nothing you can do, I will hold you as long as I like." Just then she gave a great twist to her entire body while at the same time emptying her bladder and bowels down the front of my shirt. Startled, I let her go muttering abuse about dirty little beggars who took advantage of silly little boys. I never tried to catch a mouse again.

I decided to watch the larks instead. I knew the nest where the hen was hatching her four speckled eggs. She left them for a while every day to soar, hover and sing with her mate. I lay on my back to watch them high above and when she landed she looked kindly at me seeming to say, "thanks for not touching my eggs." The snipe too had a nest with her eggs but she sounded dangerous with her goat-call as she dived, better keep my distance. The curlew and the snipe have to lay long eggs to make room for the chick's long bills.

The thrush had her nest with four scalded chicks in a whitethorn bush a hundred yards from the road. Her problem was that she fed them newly shelled snails but the only stone available for breaking the shells was on the road. One day I carried a stone from the road and left it near her nest. She always used it and never went to the road again. The chicks soon got their feathers and flew away.

The stork stands on one leg in the shallow part of the river, waits for passing fish that he grabs and swallows head first. You can see the shape of the whole fish making a moving bulge in the long neck as it swallows. It's silly to say that the stork could bring babies, as he is barely able to take off with no weight at all.

The beetles were the best sport. Using my stick and hands, I dug a round hole six inches deep and four inches across in a cow-track. The peaty clay was black and damp and I patted the inside of the hole smooth. Then I sprinkled dry dusty clay around the walls. Into this hole I put beetles, black, green, fat, thin and some very long that could lift up their heads. When they tried to creep out of the hole the loose dust gave way and they fell back in. The green ones were small and fast and clearly thought speed would carry them up and sometimes they moved their legs so fast they kicked all the loose dust away and when they found good footing and they escaped. The big black ones on the other hand took things slowly and carefully but seldom escaped. At the end of the game I threw them a fist full of grass as a ladder to get out.

Another good game was a snail race. I had a piece of timber that I found on the road and when I put a number of snails in the middle of it I could watch to see which one slides to the edge first on his silvery trail. Snails have little horns that they can retract if there is any danger. Their eyes seem to be on the top of those, as they cannot travel if they are retracted. By holding a finger over one emerging horn a snail can be steered in any direction. So you could have an off the board race or a straight-line race. If there were two people you could have a snail each and compete but as I was always alone I had a race with my right hand against my left hand.

Pakie used to cycle past to his dinner and back and just say hello but when he was going home from work in the evening he sometimes stopped for a chat. I told him one day about my fear of aeroplanes and my air raid shelter. He laughed and said "Do you think the Germans have nothing better to do than bomb a snotty nosed "gossen" in a callow?" They were the sweetest words I ever heard, as they took a load of my mind.

The Mission

Since our voices were beginning to break, we were ordered to the men's mission. The annual parish mission ran Sunday-to-Sunday inclusive, one week for the men and the following week for the women. The sermon on this, the Wednesday night, was on "Company Keeping". This, the most important sermon of the week was given by the old man. The young man gave gentle sermons about prayer and devotion; the middle-aged man who was big, burly and gruff gave more robust sermons about rowdiness, drunkenness, honesty and easy things like that.

We knew absolutely nothing about company keeping but we were highly motivated and keen to learn. In fact we hoped to start practical trials as soon as possible and any tips or guidelines would be greatly appreciated. That's why we had looked forward to this night as we expected to gain valuable information while being told what "not to do". We assumed that the louder and more thunderous the exhortations, the more informative it might be. We did fear hell and the wrath of God but we expected to live long lives in which to repent and now our needs were pressing.

"The quiet road, the lonely road, is the broad road to destruction," that's how he started off. It sounded promising. "The only worse den of iniquity is the cinema." The only time we had been to the pictures was a matinee about The Song of Bernadette. We saw no iniquity there. We had no idea what iniquity meant but from the sound of things it must have something to do with forbidden pleasure. Dens were resting places in long grass for certain wild animals, hares and the like. Maybe if you went company keeping in such a place that would be iniquity. Or it might lead to iniquity. We were anxious to hear more. We sure did hear more!

"In those dens of iniquity you have titillation on the screen and temptation in the stalls," he thundered. "Wow!" There was a word and a half. What did it mean? How did it work? It sounded exciting. Did you do it yourself or with someone else or to someone else, or did someone do it to you? Its possibilities were endless. Talk about entertaining bad thoughts! This was beyond our wildest dreams. We had a whole parlour full of bad thoughts here. We would need to live to a hundred years to get over all these thoughts. Our minds were so over-worked that we sailed into a sort of trance and totally lost track of the sermon or the holy man delivering it. That's what happened me anyway and I suppose it was the same for my pals Algie and Jimmy. They sat on my right, beside the centre aisle while on my left was an austere old gentleman who had hung his walking stick on the back of the seat in front of us. He was antagonistic from the start, when sash-wearing ushers made him move in to make room for us; he scowled but held his peace. We were barely on time and grinning as we shuffled in beside him, if looks could kill?

Dreaming through my thoughts, I was dimly aware of the preacher telling of some old mystic who had a vision of a great sinner's conscience, right throughout his totally unrepentant life. He was disobedient as a child and showed no remorse he droned. Immediately in front of us was a dark haired young man who had just got a haircut, short back and sides. This was obvious as his neck was weather beaten except for a half inch white line bordering his hair. He had probably been on the bog all week. Just then I spotted a head-louse emerging from under his collar and heading for the new neat hairline. I elbowed Algie and pointed out the creeper with my eyes.

"A penny says he gets scratched off before he reaches the hairline," I said out of the side of my mouth. Without reply he covered the penny I had placed on the seat between us. The old man threw a sidelong dirty look. We tried to look rapturously engrossed in the sermon. We did listen a bit and by now the unrepentant scoundrel was defiling young girls and still no remorse. The louse was now more than half way across the open space and my penny was sweating. At that time there were lice in every house, except ours! As the louse reached his target and Algie reached for the pennies,

"Doubles or quits he doesn't reach cover," said I as I put down another two pennies. There was a small chink, another dirty look and more angelic stares. This looked a good option for me as the louse was struggling in the new stubble and the cover was a good two inches away. By now the scoundrel in the sermon was stealing from his employer and going on drunken orgies and still, no remorse. Instead of scratching, the man with the louse began to nod off and his head tilted forward making the going easier for the insect and further endangering my bet.

Having smashed all of the Ten Commandments with total defiance and no trace of remorse the scoundrel was now dead and lying in his coffin at his own wake. People were supping drinks and trying with great difficulty, to recall something good to say about him, when suddenly the corpse roared out, "I am damned." This brought everyone in the church to attention. Our nodding louse-man sat bolt upright, twitching his stubble neck and sending the louse soaring in the air. I had won my bet.

My joy was short lived. The louse landed right in the fly of Algie's trousers. There were no zips in those days. He gave an almighty "bunnogue" (an awkward panic-stricken sideways lurch) putting the pennies and the old mans stick clattering on to the floor. Anybody would think that it was a lion, not a louse that was threatening his prized possessions. I just could not contain the belly laugh. The problem was that I had just gained control of my new big voice but the laugh was only half there. It started off falsetto, going very deep and back falsetto, altogether like a demonic sneer of unearthly origins. There was a great turning of heads and general rustle. Oh God help me I was in deep trouble. I urged Algie and Jimmy to make a run for it. By now the old man had recovered his stick and was poking me behind and hissing about sacrilegious young blackguards who needed the devil beaten out of them.

The preacher continued, pretending not to notice the commotion but the young missioner was heading down in our direction and the middle-aged man, coming from the rear, cut off our retreat. I was facing the death penalty, or at least excommunication. I decided to blame the louse! Now I knew how Eve must have felt when blaming the snake.

"What is the meaning of this?" The big man demanded.

"It all started when he shouted, I am damned," I stuttered. He looked down at Algie, still clutching his valuables.

"My goodness" he said,

"Was he frightened into an accident?"

"Take him out," he said, in a much more conciliatory tone. As we shuffled down the aisle, I thought,

"Oh thank you God, you really did come to save sinners." Algie was petrified, Jimmy was mortified, and I was satisfied, having my sentence commuted to a fourpenny fine and a sore behind. And the louse! He just married locally and lived happily ever after.

The Summer of '43

"It looks like the war is turning against the Germans," that's what the men said after Mammy read the paper last night. They were talking in the firelight as Mammy blew out the lamp as soon as she finished reading in order to spare the paraffin oil. As always she stood up on a chair, put her hand sideways at the top of the globe and blew. It seemed very dark for a minute but when your eyes got used to the darkness you could see well enough by the flickering firelight. Stories about the war were scarier in the dark but not as scary as ghost stories. As long as I can remember, Germany was always winning and they were able to run through other countries in a few weeks, isn't that very strange? Or maybe James was right when he said "Russia would stop them just like it stopped Napoleon."

"Who the hell was Napoleon?" asked Jim,

"Or what has he to do with the war?"

"He was a French man who like Hitler thought he would take over the world. He was going great until he brought his army of over a million soldiers to Russia where most of them died with the cold. History repeats itself they say."

"That was before the panzer car was invented, it would not happen now," said Peter. James was very old. He told me he was seventy-six years older than me and he remembered back to the eighteen sixties. Peter says that old man is doting half the time and not to give him any heed but he had good stories and he knew about the war.

"Your father, Larry, was a great orator," that's what James said. "In nineteen eighteen after the British had executed the men of nineteen sixteen, the Sinn Fein party was formed to fight the general election. The party people at that

ORIGINAL IRISH STORIES

time asked me and your father to write suitable speeches to convince everybody to take courage and vote out the British altogether. All those standing were new people many of them were wanted by the police, indeed half of them were in jail, (put there by the Sassenach). When big meetings took place and they were very big, because the British had turned everyone against them with the 1916 executions, the speakers would be watched by the peelers and might be arrested or harassed some time later. Many of them were arrested and held on some charge or other, just to keep them out of circulation until after the election. The peelers wouldn't dare step in while the crowd was there but a day or two later when all was quiet that's when they'd pounce. They were very sneaky that way.

"After a while Sinn Fein got round this by sending their orators to other constituencies where they would not be recognized. Good speakers were scarce and the message had to be got to everybody in Ireland within a few weeks. This could only be done by orators speaking loud and clear to large crowds for up to an hour at a time to get the message across. The whole idea was new. Only dreamers thought of a free Ireland before this time and if Sinn Fein failed at this election while the people's blood was up they would never get the chance again. That's why speakers were prepared to go on the run in a strange part of the country and sleep in a different safe house every night.

"O'Nael was involved in organizing this. His real name was William O'Neill but everybody called him O'Nael. He had a very fast pony and sidecar and on this he took your father on a three week speaking tour of Galway seeking votes for Kevin O'Higgins. He brought his little son Christy with him as well so that people would think they were local. They went the coach road through Ballinasloe. In Clonark they met the gentry (Naghtens) taking the crown of the road and it went very hard on O'Nael to give way. "Keep your cool William," said Larry,

"After we win this election they will come to know their place." After the three weeks travelling through Galway the peelers were watching for them so they decided to come home by Ballyforan. A friend of theirs took the sidecar and child across the bridge together with a few of his own children, just to fool the watching peelers. After dark the two men crossed by boat a mile downriver. From there locals led them through fields of rocks and ferns 'till they reached Fallons in Coolderry near Dysart where their sidecar and child and a great feed were waiting, served by Liza and Mariah. They stayed there for the night and came home very early the following morning, Election Day. They came through Drum to avoid the barracks in Bealnamulla. Your father got off at Killians and came home the Mass path while O'Nael returned to Mounthussey. Later that day both men went to vote in Drum school as if they were there all the time. Sinn Fein won the election and declared Ireland a free state and that's how we finally got rid of the British. They still have the six counties but we will get them back as well, if not in my time, certainly in yours."

Old James died in 1941 and while his prophecy has not yet come to pass, things have changed for the better and hopefully I have a little more time!

The Wagtail

The wagtail walks with dignity
A tailored morning suit wears he
With waggling tail and eyes of glee
He is a merry sight to see.

He walks about at early morn
With eyebrows raised o'er eyes that scorn
The sun his plumage does adorn
As he disdains to perch on thorn.

He is the bane of all small birds
He bosses them in other words
He uses beak and vocal cords
And so o'er others all he lords.

He is a lover too of sex
Sweet maidens hearts he cruelly wrecks
Each mound that's raised he proudly decks
All challengers he soundly pecks.

And yet his pride, his grace, his glee,
His charm, his cheek, his dignity,
Would fall to bits if he should see
The girl who's going to marry me.

Woolworth's

Smart, well-travelled people, who had been to Dublin, knew all about Woolworth's nick-knack shop. They sold everything under the sun, from a needle to an anchor. Anybody who had never been there was backward. Then, wonderful news arrived. They were going to open a shop in our town. Even the war, the rationing and the coupons could not dampen our enthusiasm at the great news. They had acquired the building, work on its renovation was proceeding, and it would be open for Christmas. Santa Claus would be there, we had heard, but we did not really believe that he visited the Dublin shop every year. Now we could see for ourselves. Just because you were only seven didn't mean you were stupid.

When the sign over the new shop went up everybody said that the spelling was wrong, "Wellworths." They supposed it would be noticed and put right by next week but it wasn't. Instead we heard that it was not the real Woolworth's at all but a copycat company. However they would have many of the same things, nearly as good. The question was would they have packs of small playing cards selling for sixpence. A full size pack cost a half a crown. "Haven't ye your father's playing cards, aren't they good enough?" That's what Mammy said. Daddy's playing cards were several years old and there were only thirty-seven left out of the original pack and even those were in poor condition. They were dog-eared and marked so that many of them were recognisable from the back. This led to cheating by the older members of the family.

I had learned to count on the cards long before I went to school. There were forty-five in the pack then. I heard there were several games you could play if you had all fifty-two cards but we had only two games, strip-jack (beg of my neighbour) and casino. Only two could play strip-jack, so casino was usually played. In this game every player got four cards and there were four cards placed face up on the table. If the first player had a card in his hand matching one on the table, he could put both in his bank. Sometimes he could pick two or three cards off the table, if their number added up to a card in his hand, for instance a two a three and a four could be picked up by saying two plus three plus four equals my nine. He could then put all four cards in his bank. If he had no match he just had to leave down a card. Deals continued until all the cards were gone and whoever had the biggest bank won.

When my aunt gave me sixpence in town, during the Christmas week that Wellworth's opened, I decided to look for the little playing cards. That was the first day Santa was there and the crowds were huge. Behind the two girls at the door there was a long queue of children and parents and at the end of the line was a fake Santa. I might have been only seven years old but everybody knew Jim Farrelly. One of the door girls grabbed me.

"Give me your shilling and then you can join the queue for Santa." I glared at her.

"I don't want to go to Santa I just want a pack of playing cards for my six pence."

"You cannot go to Santa unless you have a shilling."

"I don't want to go to Santa," and I ducked under her arm and ran down the shop with her after me. The manageress appeared,

"What's all the fuss?"

"He won't line up for Santa."

"I want a pack of playing cards and I only have sixpence." She took the sixpence and gave me the most beautiful little box with a king of diamonds on the outside. Now it was the door girl's turn to glare.

"Now! We'd see who would cheat, who would claim that three and four was eight, who would read the backs of the cards. The owner of the cards would call the tune. Anybody caught cheating would be put out of the game. It was great to be a man in charge of his own cards.

Tricky Dúbh

A year after her husband's death in 1927 it became clear that the widow was on the lookout. Three serious suitors were quickly into the ring, after all her late husband, Kieran, had left her with a snug twenty acres and a house built into the shelter of a cut-away hill. Thatch would last twice as long in this sheltered position.

Of course one couldn't show ones hand too soon as failure with one woman would hinder ones chances in future. Funny, the way everyone fancied the same woman while others could get no man at all. Then again twenty acres had it's own beauty. Rambling in at night for a chat was the most widespread leisure activity at the time and a man with intentions could call as a rambler without totally revealing those intentions. After an hour alone with the widow a man might broach the subject. Paddy Bán (fair), John Dearg (red) and Tricky Dúbh (black) all had the same idea. That's why all three spent every night rambling in the widow's house this sherraft. Sherraft was the period between Christmas and Lent and was the time for weddings. While their nicknames once indicated their hair colour, now in their fourth decade there was little difference between them. As none had farms of their own this might well be their last throw of the romantic dice.

Paddy Bán was a laidback, dreamy, romantic chap whom a woman could love but his farming abilities were suspect. His experience with the opposite sex was all in his head. John Dearg was a go-getter who would skin a flea and skin anybody else who got in his way. Some people called him "John skin the goat". The woman who got him would never be short of a few bob even if she were never at liberty to spend it. His only previous romantic encounter had ended abruptly when it transpired that the object of his affections did not own the uncles farm after all. Tricky Dúbh who was from a wealthier family was gracious and charming but was something of a black sheep who had earned his nickname. His romantic encounters were many and varied and indeed there were rumours of a scandal or two.

As Ash Wednesday approached all became more desperate and competition increased at the nightly meetings. A four-way conversation is not an ideal forum for suitors, especially if there is only one lady. A man has to measure his words so as to belittle the others without appearing vindictive. It's not easy to get to portray one's assets, one's physical powers, one's charms, one's charisma, or one's manhood while in the presence of two jealous rivals. All comments are likely to be misconstrued, added to, laughed at, sneered at or generally belittled.

Then, on the Friday before Ash Wednesday the morning was the wettest for many years. If a man got very wet out looking for a stray calf wouldn't it be reasonable for him to seek temporary shelter in the house of an acquaintance and if that acquaintance happened to be the widow with whom a man wanted to have a serious private conversation so much the better.

Whether it's that great minds think alike or that fools seldom differ I could not say, but all three suitors had the same idea around daylight on the morning in question. John Dearg and Tricky Dúbh jumped out of bed and prepared to look the part. They would need to walk in the rain for half an hour to look suitably wet. John Dearg, not to be wasteful, went to the well for water making sure to splash himself so as to look wet. Tricky Dúbh herded the widow's livestock at the back of her house. Paddy Bán stayed in bed for a while to think. If he had this great idea maybe the others had it too. He got dressed, shaved and went as far as the ivy clad tree a hundred yards north of the widow's house. He would watch from there for a while.

As Tricky Dúbh was approaching the house from the back he spotted John Dearg coming up the south road. He hid behind the haycock where the goat was suckling her two kids. About the time John Dearg was reaching the front door, he took the ladder from the haycock, placed it against the low thatched roof, grabbed a kid and climbed up to the chimney. Up the wide chimney came the voice of John Dearg calling, "God save all here," Just then he dropped the kid down the chimney. The frightened beast upturned the kettle off the crane, the toast off the tongs, put the fire flying round the kitchen, and broke two willow pattern plates from the dresser before escaping out the door. In her fright and confusion the widow thought that John Dearg had brought the goat. Where else could it have come from? Picking up the twig she attacked John Dearg physically and verbally, raining blows on him while calling him obscene names and ordering him out of her house. Not knowing where the kid came from, he was shocked by the whole episode and ran for his life. As he struggled home through the rain, his heart and spirit broken he muttered to himself, what was the weird woman doing with the goat? Were there things about women and goats he did not know? Now he would never know. If that's the sort of them then he didn't want to know. They could all go to hell and the sooner the better.

"What on earth happened here?" said Tricky Dúbh as he watched the widow picking up the bits of willow pattern plates?

"They were my grandmother's," she wailed

"And look at the fire all over the floor and my toast, that lunatic John Dearg brought a goat into the house and a mad goat at that."

"A goat is it? The sign of the devil, you'll have to get the house blessed, I always had my doubts about poor John, and you're lucky to be rid of him. Here let me help you tidy up."

"Why did you throw the kid goat down the chimney?" That's what Paddy Bán said as he came in.

"What are you talking about?" Said Tricky Dúbh.

"I saw you throwing the goat down the chimney."

The widow went for the twig again, this time with more ferocity, indeed Tricky Dúbh was lucky to escape with his life.

After Tricky Dúbh left Paddy Bán had the field to himself. Their descendants are still around, no longer Bán or dreamy as the widow's dusky beauty and spirited personality changed all that.

The Thunderstorm

"Gather up your cows and bring them home now," that's what Pakie said as he walked past very fast on his way home from work.

"But it's only six o'clock yet and I don't bring them home until eight."

"There's lightning and thunder coming, so bring them home now and you might make it before the rain". I think he changed it to rain because he saw that I was frightened of the lightning and thunder. Then he hurried on walking very fast. If he was hurrying like that it looked bad for me because I had farther to go than him and I had to get the cattle from the far end of the callow. If I ran very fast and beat them on with my stick I might make it. Off I ran as fast as I could but the cows knew it was early and I had to run from one side of the field to the other beating them on one at a time as they thought I was daft bringing them home this early. There had been no wind all day but now there was a sort of strong whirlwind, warm and blustery, sort of going all directions at once. Was this a fairy blast? It certainly was eerie.

Then I heard the first rattle of thunder rolling up from the bottom of the sky to a spot over Lennon's shop. I had to pass that way so I would meet the shower on the road. Then there was a great zigzag flash of lightning, that must be fork lightning and fork lightning is more dangerous. Oh! Oh! The thunder was rolling up the sky again, higher and nearer this time and much, much louder. I had barely got the cattle out on the road when the rain started, huge drops, bigger than I'd ever seen before. The lightning flashes were one after another now and the thunder rolled one on top of the other. I beat the cattle into a run but I could not hear myself shouting at them with the noise of the thunder. Then the rain was running down my face so fast that I could not draw my breath without turning my face to the ground to keep the stream of water off my mouth and nose. My braces began to stretch, as my old trousers got heavy with water. I was the third person to grow into these trousers and the many patches on the backside were now making it very heavy. That's what comes from sliding down the hay-shifter. This morning the dry sand was running between my toes but now the road already had a sheet of water, deep enough to cover my toes. Lucky I was in the bare ones, (wearing no footwear). As we started up the hill to the trees the water got deeper under my feet, it was up to my ankles now and the torrents were tearing the gravel from under my feet and the lightning was very near. The thunder was now a tearing sound and I could smell the raw sulphur smell of the lightning. Would the next flash hit me? I was seven years old and I had just made my First Communion. I would say my communion prayers. I give Thee my body that it may be chaste and pure. I think chaste means clean and even behind my ears is clean now with all the heavy rain and my feet, which are always dirty, are definitely washed now. I give Thee my soul that it may be free from sin. There's a cow-dung after passing in the torrent but it's washed away now. I can't think of any sins now so I suppose I'm all right. I give Thee my heart that I may always love Thee. I suppose I do love You. You look a nice little fellow in your Mother's arms. I give Thee every breath that I shall breathe, "As if I could stop." Hadn't I to turn my face to the road a minute ago to get my breath. And especially my last; maybe this is my last if the next flash hits me. I might turn into a little cherub and I could fly above the cows and beat them on. But then I'd be naked and the people in the shop would laugh at me. I give Thee myself in life and in death that I may be Thine forever and ever. What am I talking about? Aren't You in total charge already? Isn't it You who makes the lightening and thunder and the rain and everything, You can do what You like so I might as well trust You?

I didn't know that the shop was full of people crying with fear and saying the rosary. Jack who was standing looking out the door saw me and shouted, come out ye bunch of cowards and see this. Faces and more faces appeared at the door and windows. Some even came out in the rain. They were laughing and crying at the same time. How was I to know that the weight of the rain had pulled all the patches off my trousers and that my backside was looking out? I was ready to die a minute ago anyway, so what did I care! I laughed too and walked on with my cows. I would never again fear death or people laughing at me.

A Game of Fifteen

1

One night in Paddy Lennon's
In dark and dreary weather
The lads were playing nine,
Each three and three together.

2

Eddie Tully, Jim and Billy,
John Lennon, Johnny, Joe.
And Shamie, Mike and Paddy
Made up the third trio.

3

The night wore on quiet dimly,
A game a piece each way,
Then came the rubber grimly
And opened up the play.

4

Then Johnny, Joe and Johnny,
They made a flying start,
But when Shamie scored a double,
It nearly broke their heart.

5

Then Eddie, Jim and Billy,
Put on a mighty spurt
And the two games that they won,
Were slick, quick, smart and curt.

6

The next great game was up,

Two tens and just one trick,

John Lennon was the dealer

And he dole them none too quick

7

For Jim was ten already,

So were the Johns and Joe

While Shamie, Mike and Paddy

Were on the trick below.

8

Now Mike picked up his hand,

Saying the five is in the stock.

As Jim's hand he slyly scanned

He got a mighty shock.

9

For Jim he had the Jack,

His smile was broad and bright,

His lips to smack, saying

Nine bob is mine tonight.

10

And as he played that Jack card,

His eyes were mad alive,

But their sudden death was awful,

When John Lennon played the five.

11

The Billy was Bill Moore

The Connolly's Jim and Joe,

The Neill's were Shamie, Johnny,

Now all the names you know.

12

Then I thought of other players
And Doc Curley's wayward hat,
The Egan's Ned and Terry
And the Watson's Laurence and Pat.

13

Larry Donlon, Johnny Killion,
Hogg's, Tommy, Pat and Mike,
John Connolly, Bridie Lennon,
Tommy Tully on his bike.

14

Pake Cunniffe, Ned and Tommy,
Mickey Murray, Gavin Pat,
M J Harney, Christy, Johnny
And Pa Colleran for fast chat.

15

The Shines, P J and Mike,
Padraig Noone and brother Joe,
Pakie Neill and young Pat Connor
Replayed each Wireless Show.

16

Joe Brogan, Johnny Walsh,
Jack Macken, Paddy Lennon,
While standing at the back,
Peter Dunning and Liam Hannon.

17

Three sat upon the settle bed,
Three opposite on the form,
With two inside the counter
And the last one on the stool.

18

The table was the shutter,
An add for Players Please,
It was taken from the window
And left down upon their knees.

19

As the settle bed was higher,
And the stool some way below,
It took a man with longer legs
To level up the show.

20

Although the shop was tiny,
It was tidy, smart and neat
And the service to the shoppers
Was efficient and discreet.

An Alarm Clock

"This is your final warning, if you are late one more morning you will be dismissed." That's what the stationmaster at Kings Cross railway station said to Timmy. In 1957 Timmy had come to London with another twenty-five thousand young Irishmen. Most of the others were big, strong muscular men who were willing and able to work as navies with Wimpeys or McAlpines. Timmy alas was weak, lanky, lean and lazy.

"Avoid hard work, you're not able for it." That's what his mother always told him. In this he always obeyed her. That was why he avoided the building sites and got a job with British Rail. Now he was on his final warning.

He shared the digs with three Wimpies, a bed in each corner of the big room on the third floor. In the other big room across the hall were four big Kerry McAlpines. All eight shared the tiny kitchen, the radio, the banter and several pints each, nightly. Unfortunately Timmy's starting time was six am while the navies started at eight. Now he was on his last chance.

You need one of these alarm clocks with two bells on top with a little hammer that bangs over and back between them. Place it in a tin basin to double the noise; it would waken the dead, that's what his friends told him. Get it today, tomorrow will be too late.

He found the clock easy enough but the basin that was a different thing. If you were in Mohill or Coothill or Summerhill you'd have no bother buying a tin basin but in London you won't find a tin basin in Harrods window or any other high street window for that matter. Pronouncing it "bashin" wouldn't help your cause either. However he persisted and finally was on his way home with the basin wrapped in brown paper under one arm and the hammer clock held by its carrying handle in the other hand. Then he met the two Cavan girls, the big one and the little one, Mary and Mona. They lived next door.

"Are you going to make a bomb with the clock?" said Mary.

"Give it to me and I'll put it inside my coat."

All three got on the busy tube train, Timmy sat in the middle, the big girl sat on his right and he put the basin upside down on his left to give the small girl a lift. When she sat the basin dinged a little with a plonking sound. Unfortunately she was suffering from severe hiccups, each of which was followed by a double plonking of the basin. It would have been worse if it had been the big girl, as she had a smoker's cough.

Opposite sat two Cockney gentlemen, black taxi drivers, on their way home. They were greatly amused by the antics of the "Oirish" and one of them said to Mary as she coughed,

"Cough it up mate it might be a watch."

"No it's a clock," she said as she pulled out the clock. That shook him and all the carriage laughed loudly at him. Just as the Cockneys turned nasty with racist remarks the train stopped at the Tottenham Court Road and the three Wimpies got on and threw off the two Cockneys. That settled that.

Now that he was sure of being wakened in the morning Timmy and his friends celebrated well and fell into bed after midnight. The clock in the basin was even better than expected. At five am all hell broke loose. Timmy thought the war had started in his head, the devil of a clock was jumping round the basin clamouring for action. He picked it up and hurled it at the wall only there was no wall there, just a window. If you are driving a black taxi in London at five in the morning what are the chances of being hit by a flying clock?

When last seen Timmy was clambering over back-garden walls in Camden Town in his pyjamas pursued by a very angry taxi man.

A Part Time Farmer

As I had a ten o'clock appointment in the morning in Dungarvan, a long way from my home in Roscommon, we retired early and I was soon in slumber land. I dreamt of someone running down a stairs and making tapping noises getting louder and more annoying. Then the tapping was on the window and was no longer a dream. The clock read three fifteen.

"Who's there?"

"The head is coming and no feet," came the reply.

"Get hot water and soap and I'll be with you in a minute."

I pulled on an old pair of pants over my pyjamas, donned an ancient crombie coat saved for such an occasion and hurried to the scene of the problem.

Having discarded the crombie and pyjama top, I scrubbed up with tepid water and carbolic soap, right to the top of my arms. This was a big cow. Birth canals are designed for things to go down and things can only be pushed in the other direction in extreme emergency and amid great pain and suffering. However, needs must and there were two lives at stake here, so with great difficulty I pushed the head back and went searching for the legs. They lay along the belly of the calf and I had to reach the knee before I could start a rolling movement of the leg and shoulder to get it in the right direction and do the same again with the fetlock. At last I got one foot out. Having secured it with a rope I now had to repeat the performance in even tighter conditions for the second leg. Finally, when feet and head were lined up, the delivery was relatively easy. The big charolais bull calf seemed dead.

We caught him by the hind legs and swung him around until he cried out in pain. We then presented him to his exhausted mother who enthusiastically licked dry his poor swollen head and went into ecstasies of happy little moos when he responded with a slimy sneeze. Her pain and suffering were forgotten. Everything seemed to be all right but I knew that after all that handling she was almost certain to get a sickening, debilitating, rotten and life threatening infection. God knows she had suffered enough so I gave her an injection of twenty cubic centimetres of "Penstrep" (Penicillin/ Streptomycin). I would give her another tomorrow night. As I dried myself after scrubbing down I got paid.

"God Bless Your Gifted Hands and May you pass them on to the next generation!"

As a youth I had gained a reputation for being handy and lucky so I catered for the whole village.

Coming home along the lane way, I was treated to the dawn chorus mingled with the enchanting aroma of the whitethorn blossom. The old people used to say, it was an echo of the heavenly refrain. Man had built this lane and the stonewalls enclosing it, but the bushes, the briars, the birds, the bees and a myriad of creepy-crawlies had ribbon built its full length in a most higgledy-piggledy fashion and without planning permission. Then I met a fox. I looked at him and he looked at me as if to say, "What the hell are you doing here at this hour of the morning, invading my space?" His family and my family had grudgingly shared those lands for three hundred years. Of course his family and the families of the ribbon builders were probably here twenty times that long. There was also The Right Honourable RamPotts family, absentee English landlords, who for a few hundred years extracted penal rents and thought they owned estates in Connaught.

Having showered shaved and downed a good breakfast, I set off for Dungarvan. I crossed the Shannon at Shannonbridge, the Brosna and the Grand Canal at Clonony, the Camcor at Birr and the river Mall at Roscrea before crossing the River Suir for the first time at Thurles. I followed the Suir valley all the way to Clonmel where I turned right and crossed the river for the last time. I then went the scenic route, round the hills to where the "old oak tree" of song overlooks Dungarvan. To me, an inlander, it was breathtakingly beautiful nestling in the great sea that stretched away to the horizon and beyond to France.

This is where I called into a country shop, one of those places that sell everything. A department inspector was just prosecuting the owner for selling country eggs.

"It is an EEC regulation," he said.

"That all eggs have to go through proper channels and be officially weighed, graded and stamped before being offered for sale. Otherwise, we have no way of knowing where those eggs might have come from."

I tentatively suggested that they probably came from a hen.

Well! He turned on me like a soot drop.

"Do you realise that it is illegal to interfere with an EEC official in the course of his duty?" He then requested a heavily pregnant young Bán Garda to arrest me. I apologised profusely as I did not want my delivery services called on twice in one day. Enough said.

The Ghost Story

It was a frosty night in January in the year of Our Lord nineteen hundred and nine. Bill was the church caretaker in this half parish. The priest only rode his horse out here on Sunday to read Mass or for funerals. This was one such day as this evening the remains of old Granny Smith had come to the chapel. Coffins were left in the back of the chapel overnight. He had locked the church earlier at ten and had only come out to look at the cows before going to bed. It was just after midnight. Was that a noise he heard in the church?

It couldn't possibly be as he had barred the double doors on the inside before exiting through the sacristy door, which he locked with the key. Why he still had it in his pocket. Just the same, it was only twenty yards to the double doors, he would have a look. Halfway there he felt a bit eerie so he called out.

"Is there anyone there?" The only reply he got was a creaking door. As he moved into the shadow he could see that one of the double doors was half open. What the hell? He stopped in his tracks. He peeped in the door, he could not see, he pushed in the door a bit farther. He looked over to where the coffin was left on trestles. Good God! The old woman was sitting up in the coffin. He could see her by the moonlight that came through the stained glass windows. He could feel his hair stand on end. She had her head on the end of the coffin with her two arms hanging over the sides. The lid of the coffin was standing up against a pillar.

"Did that lid move?" He thought it did.

"Don't be daft he told himself, coffin lids don't move of their own accord. There, it moved again, it had feet, little bare feet." He looked back to the coffin. It had legs, two bare legs. Had the old woman put her legs down through the bottom of the coffin? The legs had a white shroud dangling to the knees. Bill was rooted to the spot. Sheer terror froze him. Then a white cowl appeared over the edge of the coffin. He felt its eyes peering.

A great unearthly shriek emanated from the cowl. It sounded like r-u-n-f-o-r y-o-u-r l-i-f-e. So screaming, the white ghost emerged from behind the coffin and headed straight for Bill at the open door. A black ghost who came from behind the lid chased him. Bill collapsed into the back seat just in time to avoid been trampled on by the screaming ghosts. They went through the opening like bats out of hell. Had he really collapsed? Or did they run through him? He just didn't know any more. He was glad that the shrieks were receding into the distance. He hoped he had seen the last of them. His hair was still on end. It had probably turned white.

A few people who lived near the road thought they heard screaming, but they could not be sure. Some thought they dreamt it. Not so John and Stephen who were coming home with a good few pints on them. They saw the ghosts all right. They passed them on the road at great speed. Their shrieks had subsided by then. They disappeared after crossing the dragon stream, near old Granny Smith's house. John spent the rest of his life, which wasn't very long, mumbling in a drunken haze. Stephen on the other hand took the pledge the very next day and never drank again for the remaining thirty years of his life. Indeed, it was rumoured that he confided to his good wife that he saw the devil chasing his soul across the dragon stream and that he promised God that if he gave him another chance, he would never drink again.

Meanwhile back at the church, Bill sat in a trauma trance, silently invoking God, His Blessed Mother and every saint in creation. Eventually, his heart slipped back out of his mouth and began to beat normally, his hair lay down again and the sweat all over his body began to cool. Some of his reason returned. The small stipend he received as church caretaker made the difference between him being a poor small farmer and a very poor small farmer. His "gossans" were serving Mass and doing well at school. He might even make a priest out of one of them yet. That would give him real stature in the parish. Fear or no fear, he had to keep his job and that meant keeping the church locked and corpses in their coffins. He got up, his knees were shaking, his hands were shaking, yet he closed the double oak doors, the handles of which were u-shaped made to line up with similar u-shapes on the frames when the doors were closed. Into those slots he dropped the six by three polished oak plank that was made for the purpose. This made the whole thing rock solid. Hopefully it would keep out the ghosts if they returned.

He then went to the coffin, put back the arm on the right, walked round, put back the other arm, then down to the foot where he caught the two ankles and pulled the old woman back into the coffin. Her head bounced off the bottom with a thud, no lining in the coffins of the poor, not even a fist full of sawdust. He then rearranged her habit just for decency. He peered behind the lid, just in case, then picked it up and put it on the coffin. The wooden dowels for holding it on were under the trestles; he put them in position, pulled off one boot to tap them home. He replaced the boot. Now for the walk up the full length of the church to the sacristy.

He could not look both sides at once and ghosts might emerge from the shadows of the seats at any time. The red sanctuary lamp looked down; its dull light mingling with the dim moonlight making the whole scene eerie, unreal, ghostly even.

He could hear his own breathing, his heart was pounding again, the sound of his own footsteps unnerved him, but finally he reached the sacristy. He rushed in, unlocked the outer door, dashed out and locked the door behind him. He had done his duty. He would keep his job. Nobody would ever know what happened here.

Having broken the ice on the barrel under the eve, he washed death from his hands, wiped them in his trousers and tiptoed back into his house. Everybody was still asleep. He had not been missed. As he crept into bed beside his sleeping wife his courage and reason returned. Why had the ghosts left the dowels under the trestles? Had they intended to replace the lid? If so, why? Why were they so small? Perhaps they were not ghosts at all. The Granny had only been rescued from the poor house because of the new five-shilling old age pension. By the time they had brought her home ten miles on the ass's cart she had the rattles in her throat. She died the next day. One five-shilling pension was all they got. It wouldn't half pay for the drink at the wake. And another thing! He had heard that the she was laid out on a linen sheet on the kitchen table. No one belonging to them ever owned a linen sheet, no, nor even a flour bag sheet. That's where unrestrained young love led to, poverty and want. Where would they have got the sheet? Where! Only on loan from their cousin who worked in the big house? It would have to be returned even if, through drink or pride the undertaker was allowed to put it in the coffin with the old woman. If two grandchildren hid in the church wrapped in granny's black shawl they could remove the sheet when everyone was in bed. If they were disturbed in their weird work, might they not have wrapped themselves in the sheet and the shawl and run screaming from the scene? Had he solved the puzzle? He would confront the children after the funeral tomorrow and confirm his suspicions. Until he had talked to the children he would not mention any of this to a soul. He had a long wait. He would never be sure.

The children weren't at the funeral, sick, someone said. He supposed they got cold in the church, he would see them at Mass on Sunday. They didn't come, still sick? He never saw them again. Consumption took them with the blooming of the daffodils, only twelve hours apart. They were buried together beside the Granny.

"Maybe it was ghosts that night after all. Maybe it was the children. Maybe, just maybe they should have let the dead rest? Maybe just maybe we should do the same?"

May they all stay resting in peace!

Emigrant's Return

A hundred years it took her to return,
The gentle hearted maiden from Clonown
She sailed across the world to make her life,
When times were hard and life was full of strife.
Her name she changed from Agnes, May, to Frances,
All three in fruitful marriage took their chances.
Her name, her race, her nation all were altered,
But the wistful Irish manner never faltered.
The poise, the gentle manner and sweet smile,
Through races, years and places still beguile.
Though she and all she knew have passed and gone,
Serene and ladylike she still lives on.

Eighteen year old Agnes Dunning emigrated from Clonown to Australia in 1881, Her grand daughter, Frances Padoski came to Ireland looking for her roots in 1981 and found twenty-two second cousins, to one of whom, my wife Evelyn, she bore a remarkable resemblance.

Confession

"Bless me Father for I have sinned, I sort of stole nearly two loads of hay."

"What do mean you sort of stole nearly two loads of hay? You either stole them or you didn't."

"Well I didn't exactly steal the two loads of hay, it was more that I stole nearly the price of them."

"Now look here my good man, begin at the beginning and tell me the whole story."

"Well Father, this very morning I brought a load of hay to the market with my brown Clydesdale mare. I was hoping to get four pounds for it but I'd take three-ten or even three, but when I was approached by a dandy little British army officer, I asked for six pounds."

"Now look here Paddy," says he,

"Five pounds is the maximum I can pay as I must obey the Major."

"As he was about to move off I agreed to take it." Captain Peckingham was his name, that's what he signed on the docket. It was his first week in Ireland he said as he gave instructions that I should present myself and my load of hay to Corporal Smith at the back gate office, which was in front of the hay-sheds, inside the Barracks. I sold them hay two years ago, in nineteen eighteen.

"Well Paddy," said Corporal Smith; "you got a load of "ay" for me then mate?"

"I have surely," says I, "and a little something for yourself," as I handed him a small little pint bottle of pooteen. I didn't bother to tell either of them, that my name was Willie. The corporal uncorked the bottle and took a slug!

"That's pretty lethal stuff you got there, Paddy," he said and took another slug.

"Take your ease there," says I, "just sign the docket for me and I will empty the load myself."

He signed without a demur, as by now he was fairly merry. Having tied my mare in the hayshed, I brought my signed docket to the paymaster. As the paper work was in order he handed out a big white five-pound-note. They had recently put an extension on the hay-shed that obscured the back gate from the office. As the Corporal was busy with his drink and nobody else cared, I just led my mare, complete with load, out the back gate and on up to Connaught street.

Peetie had a bar and grocery shop in Connaught Street and a yard at the back where customers could stable their horses or asses. I pulled in to this yard, where I met big Ned who was stabling a fine black gelding.

"Could I borrow your horse for an hour?" says I,

"This mare of mine is a bit skittish for crossing the town."

"You can surely, but first tell Peetie to keep me in porter until you come back."

"He is very fond of the sup but too tight too drink his own." I agreed, what else could I do? We switched the horses and I set off for the hay market again. The little Captain was still there.

"How did you get back with another load so quickly Paddy?"

"Sure my brother was waiting for me with this load at the top of Connaught Street, you see he's a bit easy going and the traffic in Queen Street would be too much for him."

"I think all you Paddies are easy going, if we had you in his Majesty's army for a few months we'd whip you into shape."

"Pity you wouldn't whip the Black-and Tans into shape," I thought to myself, but held my whist.

"Same price, same procedure," he said as he handed me another docket.

"If his pains aren't too bad my old father might send my sister with a third load," I said as I moved off.

"I may still be here," he replied.

Corporal Smith was half way in the bottle when I arrived.

"Just give me the docket to sign," he said,

"You know what to do."

"Right you be, I repeated the hay-shed charade, collected another five-pound note and took my load of hay back to Peetie's yard. There was no one about so I searched the stables but all I could find was a jennet. I gave two corner boys six pence to help me switch Ned's horse for the jennet. Ned was three sheets in the wind inside the bar and knew nothing of the goings-on in the yard. The jennet had a narrow old arse on him and wasn't able to fill the rump shape the horses had left in the load of hay. We had to make a sort of mattress with a corn sack, filled four inches thick with hay to fill out the space."

"You got a smaller load this time Paddy," said the Captain.

"Oh no," says I,

"It's just as big a load, with a smaller animal."

"Pull the other one Paddy, four pounds and count yourself lucky", he said as he wrote the docket.

"The stupid little bastard couldn't see it was the same load of hay."

"Lucky for you he couldn't and you have no right to question his parentage."

"Sorry Father."

Just as I was moving off the Captain said,

"Hold on a minute Paddy, why have you padding on the mules back?"

"Sure he'd kick the stars if a wisp of hay touched his skin," I said.

"He swallowed that."

"But you said it was a jennet you had?" said the priest.

"Would a "Sassenach" know the difference?"

"I suppose not."

"Corporal Smith was three quarter way into the bottle and was looking very grey round the gills. I had to hold his hand to sign the docket. This time I emptied the load and spread it around fairly well in case Captain Woodpecker would check it."

"I thought you said his name was Peckingham?"

"That was before he came to Ireland Father."

"Quite! But how do you justify stealing the hay?"

"Haven't we our own elected government and them and their hungry horses have no right to be here at all."

"So you see yourself as a sort of freedom fighter then?"

"I suppose you could say that."

"Normally, I would order you to return the money, but in the circumstances you can keep it, provided you give a substantial donation to the local Vincent-De-Paul."

"I will Father, I will."

"The playing fields of Eton are no match for your peasant cunning, for your penance, say a decade of the Rosary."

"There was something else Father."

"What else?"

"It was John-Joe's Maureen that filled the load of hay with me."

"Go on."

"Well when I got down off the load, there she was, after the banter and her exertions, elated, hot and happy, with the white hayseed hopping on her dark dancing curls and the love light "lepping" in her lovely laughing eyes. What was a man do?"

"Control himself! Were you cavorting in the hay?"

"Does cavorting mean rolling Father?"

"It does and were you?"

"We were a bit Father."

"And were you both fully dressed during this activity?"

"We were at the beginning Father, but things might have slipped a bit."

"You dirty blackguard, you took advantage of the girl. Is this girl in the family way?"

"Good Lord, I hope not Father."

"You hope not, are you not absolutely certain?"

"Ah Father sure no man can be absolutely certain of anything in this life."

"Do you intend to marry this girl?"

"Sure, I'd give the whole world for the chance Father, but we're too young and our families would never agree."

"How old are you?"

"We're forty between us and I'm twenty-one."

"So she is just nineteen?"

"Yesterday Father."

"A nice birthday present you gave her."

"Ah no Father, that will be today out of the price of the hay."

"Has this girl been to confession?"

"She has Father, she went to the young priest, she was afraid to face you."

"Where is she now?"

"Below at the back of the church waiting for a lift home with me."

"When you will plunge both of you into sin again, well it won't happen, because I'll stop it. Bring that girl up to the altar, right now, where I will marry you. You can give me the price of one load of hay."

"The jennet load?"

"Certainly not, I will have a big white five-pound-note. You can say the full Rosary for your penance afterwards. I'll call up two penitents for witnesses."

After they were pronounced man and wife, Maureen turned to her new husband and said,

"My wonderful Willie, it broke my heart to have to refuse you flat last night, but didn't I tell you if you played your cards right it would never happen again. Now I'm all yours. We will share the birthday present."

"You know my lovely Maureen, the cloisters of Maynooth are no match for your feminine wiles."

They said the Rosary on the way home, among other things!

The Sheep Dog

On a recent visit to Dublin's most glamorous shopping centre I sat on a seat as my good wife entered a shop. Beside me was a real old Dubliner with a perfect old Dublin accent.

"I see you are learning to be a sheep dog," says he,

"You must be recently retired and going shopping with the wife. When she says "Sit and stay" there you remain until her return when you will get your next command."

Just then his better half came out of the shop, said, "Come" and walked on. I guffawed as I thought it was very funny. Not so his better half, she dissected me with a look.

"What's that stupid hyena laughing at?" He couldn't answer as he was bent in two, feigning asthma and trying to smother the laughter. I laughed even louder, she got madder, my new friend's asthma got worse, we were on a downward spiral here, she, in danger of exploding, he about to implode and me smothering in mirth.

"Ya ignorant culchie," she said,

"Ya aren't a wet week here when ya think ya own the place and that ya can make fun of the rest of us." I never realised before that my laugh had a culchie accent. Eventually he got to explain the funny side to her, she smiled, looked at me, said, "You just sit," and walked off.

After they left, I got thinking about what he had said. I remembered the programme "*One Man and His Dog*" where the lovely black and white dog having penned all the sheep, waits in anticipation for a stray wild young one to appear, whereupon he would bound into action and have her corralled in a minute.

"Forget it kid" it is definitely not an option. Everybody around me was texting. I could be texting too if I knew how. Nobody seemed to notice my presence. They just ignored me.

Then I noticed a little girl in a buggy looking at me. I winked at her with one eye. She winked at me with two eyes. I wiggled my nose. She put up her hand and moved her nose. I looked out over my glasses. She stuck out her tongue. I stuck out my tongue. I got a belt of a handbag!

"Dirty old paedophile," she roared as she scuttled away with the child. The child waved bye bye.

There was a mangy little Jack Russell terrier trotting up the middle of the mall, intent on where he was going. He stopped to sniff me. Was he trying to tell me something?

"Don't even think about it." The kick was accurate but late, he had marked his territory. He yelped, snarled and bit my shoe, before barking loudly and swaggering off, his tail held high, top dog style.

"Cruel bugger, you should be reported to the police," said a passing English man.

"Yo man it's cool," said a Nigerian.

"Yo man you're wet," from one of a group of laughing schoolgirls.

"Yo man you're smelly," from another schoolgirl.

I was only there half an hour and already had been called, Hyena, culchie, ignorant, old, bugger, cool, paedophile, cruel, wet, stupid, dirty and smelly. I was also assaulted, hand-bagged, ignored, threatened, winked at, waved at, texted at, roared at, laughed at, yelped at, barked at, snarled at, bitten and peed upon.

I decided to just put my head on my paws, ignore the throngs and await the master.

"Come quickly or we will get caught in the rush hour traffic, we've wasted enough time here already."

John Paul II

He spoke in every language in words so clear and true,
Christ's message he explained to men of every hue.
He spoke in every country in words they understood,
And gave the gospel message as his charisma could.

He was gifted by his maker to make the good news plain,
And each who heard him thought I too could try again.
Without the power of speech he waved his suffering to us all
When like Christ upon the cross, he gave his greatest speech of all.

He gave hope to all the old, decrepit, feeble or infirm,
He showed them how to die and in heaven join with him.
Now we know there's no one useless even to their final breath,
For his deathbed message mattered to all upon this earth.

He'll be in our hearts forever for his goodness came to stay,
And his peace will dwell within us as we go upon our way.
So don't grieve for John Paul ever but celebrate his reign,
For at the gates of heaven, we'll all meet with him again.

My Conundrums

We called him Luidhe, of course that was behind his back as he was a former heavy weight boxer and he could hit you several slaps to the face in a flash if ruffled or if you got the maths wrong. He was our maths teacher but he should have been in actuary as he was totally besotted with figures or geometry or theorems or algebra or indeed anything mathematical. He had great respect for like-minded people and almost despised all others. This must have left him a bit isolated in society and he certainly was not street wise. This was where my conundrums came into play.

As you can see, the maths classes were fraught with danger for the lazy or the mathematically weak. I had an old farmer friend who had given me a conundrum to solve almost every day of my life. One day I asked Luidhe one of the most difficult ones. He immediately cleaned the blackboard and wrote up the problem on it. Then he asked for suggestions as to how it might be solved. I knew the answer, I had got it from the old farmer, and so I pompously explained the whole thing. He was ecstatic to think that he had found a like-minded person, a kindred spirit, and a genuine maths buff. After that I was his fair-haired boy.

Of course he was not to know I was addicted to cigarettes and having no regular income I had to avail of every opportunity to feed my habit. I thought of a plan. I let be known among the fearful that I could occupy Luidhe for an entire class for a fee of ten fags, half in advance the other half on completion, just like hit-man. The next day I had my first client, a watery lad whom I had helped with sums a few times before free of charge. I now had a dilemma; would I help him with the sums or distract Luidhe? We quickly reached a compromise; I would help him with the maths for two fags or distract Luidhe for the full fee. In this way I could do better overall as I could help a number of people every day whereas the number of times distractions would work had to be limited and would only be used in an emergency. Thus was my youth misspent but I am thirty years off the cigarettes now.

The Rabbit

With our sheepdog Bruno, we chased rabbits every day. The war was on and there was money in rabbits. Of course we never caught any. After all I was only six years old and my brother Frank, just eight. The same thing happened every day. All three of us arrived in the field where the rabbits were. Bruno charged after them, barking loudly, followed by the two of us, shouting skulla-hulla. The rabbits scampered off and disappeared down their burrow at the far end of the field. Bruno tore at the mouth of the burrow, then snorted down it as if to say; that will teach you a lesson. We went home empty handed, hoping for better luck next time.

One day Frank had a brain wave. He ordered me to wait a quarter of an hour, while he took a circuitous route and entered the field from the far end, where he snuck in and sat in the mouth of the burrow. When I arrived with the dog the rabbits ran for cover as usual but when they reached the burrow they ran every way in confusion. Bruno grabbed and killed one. We were shocked, elated and ecstatic all at once. Rabbits were worth a half a crown each, we were rich.

We dressed up and headed for town, three miles away. Frank carried the rabbit and I walked alongside.

"You walk the other side," he ordered.

"It's my rabbit and I don't want anybody to think that you had anything to do with catching him," I hesitated,

"If you don't go round the other side you can go home," he said.

It was better to walk the other side of a lad with a rabbit than not walk at all, so I obeyed, reluctantly, well, not so much obeyed as agreed.

After a while he changed the rabbit to the other hand and I had to change sides again. The farther we went the oftener this happened.

"Do you want me to take one leg?" I asked.

"Well just for a while," he said,

"But if we meet anyone, you must let go immediately," I agreed, it was better to carry a rabbit a bit than not carry him at all and someone might come round a corner before he got a chance to reclaim both legs. Then, wouldn't I be a big fellow? Just then a man put his head over a wall and said, "Good gossens! Are ye off to town with yer rabbit?"

"It's my rabbit I'm only letting him hold one leg for a bit."

"And take a bit of the weight," he smiled.

"I felt very grown up and important." The man could see that I was carrying half the rabbit and indeed he probably thought I was part owner. After all seeing is believing.

Shortly after I realised why I was allowed to help. We were small boys and the rabbit was big and long. While holding his paws, we had to keep our arms bent in order to keep his head off the ground. We tried to overcome this problem by catching him above the knees but this was harder on little fingers as the legs were fat and slanty. Having covered over a mile, we reached the Spring Well road. It was a quiet, mile long road running beside the railway and there was a grass verge on both sides.

Out of necessity, we were now working as a team, swapping sides as arms tired. To conserve energy we decided to walk on the verge and let the head drag on the grass. This worked well enough but by the end of the mile the head was looking the worse for the wear. We got a drink at the spring well and sat a little while. Now for the last half-mile through the town to the butcher's shop, we had to keep the head off the road and it was very difficult, only the vision of the half crown kept us going.

The butcher was standing at the door with a knife in his hand and saw us coming. He took the rabbit, slit him with the knife, threw the entrails to a passing dog, who wolfed them down, then turned to us.

"Did ye see that? That's how you gut a rabbit and ye should have gutted him hot. Because ye didn't so he is only worth eighteen pence." He handed

Frank one and six and disappeared with the rabbit. There were thirty pence in a half-a-crown. We turned away devastated, the tears overflowing in spite of manly efforts. It was a long way home. We only got just over half the money after all our struggles. What could two small boys do?

Then luck struck. Big Peter happened to be passing.

"Why are ye crying?" He asked. We told him our story. The butcher heard the commotion and reappeared explaining the gutting problem. Big Peter said nothing, just caught him by the lapels and began to hop him up and down. He turned very pale, his explanation died away and he handed me the missing shilling. Frank said I could keep it. All is well that ends well.

Summer Love

In April as I listened to the cooing of the dove
A sweet girl took my fancy and my mind just turned to love.
Grake, grake, stand back; that's what the corncrake said.
When I was doing so nicely, I wished that bird were dead.
In May while we were strolling in the laneways of the west,
We kissed and then we cuddled and thought about the rest.
Grake, grake, stand back; that's what the corncrake said.
When I was doing so nicely, I wished that bird were dead.
In June the flowers bloomed, in the summer evening gloaming
As we embraced so tightly, our love was overcoming.
Grake, grake, stand back; that's what the corncrake said.
When I was doing so nicely, I wished that bird were dead.
In July our love was stronger and we wanted all to know,
Whenever we went walking, we went where lovers go.
Grake, grake, stand back; that's what the corncrake said,
When I was doing so nicely, I wished that bird were dead.
In August we walked by, the golden corn standing,
With vital questions asked, we reached an understanding
Grake, Grake, stand back; that's what the corncrake said,
When I was doing so nicely, I wish that bird were dead.
Grake, grake, stand back; was his call unto the wild,
In September he flew south, now we're married with a child.

Weary Walkers Wend the Weeping Way

From Ardkeenan, in Connaught to Clonmacnoise was the last ten mile weeping way of bygone ages, when the good and the great brought their loved ones to Clonmacnoise for burial, as it was believed that those buried there had a better chance of heaven.

For the benefit of the mourners, the national roads authorities of the time had a road built across the bog and a wooden bridge across the Shannon at Clonmacnoise.

No doubt, it was the original N6 as it ran east to Tara and Drogheda. A designated rest field at Nure is called "the field of the dead" to this day.

The Drum Heritage Group, resurrected this route in 1998 and in the millennium year a great walk took place on September 17th. Following a blessing at Ardkeenan, the crowd snaked its way through three dioceses (Elphin, Tuam and Clonmacnois) of meadow and moor, crossing the main road at Doohon, the Derrylahan road at Greene's and ceremoniously marched into Nure where they were greeted with applause. And while there were no palms or cloaks strewn on the road, nor was there anybody riding a donkey, one was reminded of the triumphal entry into Jerusalem.

When Edward Egan stepped forward at the little thatched morgue we felt for a moment that he might call in a loud voice, "Lazarus come forth," but instead he called on a loud-hailer,

"Jackie McManus come forward and declare this house of the dead open." He was the man who donated the land for this historic morgue.

Well, the little wake house was duly opened, blessed by Father Ray and Edward instructed his committee to seat the multitude on chairs, as the grass was wet. They did not have loaves and fishes but in the words of a local, "an ass load of sandwiches and buns". The good people of Nure threw their houses open to the public and it was just as well as many of the multitude had partaken of bottles of orange at Derrylahan and now their needs were pressing.

Having eaten and drank their fill and danced on the village green, they had a raffle before proceeding to Killumper and the ferry. Imagine, in this third millennium walking in a funeral of the first millennium and wishing God speed on their heavenly way to those so long dead. Yes, it would be irreverent to suggest that it is now not worth their while.

Unfortunately, the last ferry broke down and Edward and the last of his followers were stranded on the Connaught side. Some expected him to walk the waters, but the Shannon was angry, with a curling lip so he called on two local fishermen, cousins, Kevin and Donal O'Brien who braved the waves and took him across. Edward then said, "I will make you fishers of men. Go thence to the rain swept shores of Killumper, find my faithful followers and ferry them across to St Kieran's sacred city." They left their fishing gear and went and did his bidding.

Finally, a colourful, kilted piper led the multitude through the river field to the stile entrance to the sacred city, watched by the bemused swans and cattle whose space was invaded. Then, sitting on damp tombstones, the weary multitude had a chance to commune with God, with nature, with the elements, with their dead ancestors and with themselves. And spare a thought for St Kieran the hermit, who found his island hermitage at Lough Ree too crowded, and so, taking one helper, he sailed down the Shannon to the quiet watered land of Clonmacnoise, where, within the year he died and was buried alone, in this lonely place with the backdrop of the Clonascra hills. Could this hermit ever have envisaged that we would bury fifteen hundred years of people with him?

My Finest Hour

In the nineteen forties cutting the turf was one of the most important tasks of the year for most families. Without turf there would be no cooking or heating in the homes of Ireland. Considerable planning went into the week on the bog as this usually involved all hands, that is the entire family, from the baby in the horses collar to the daddy on the "slane". In between were the little girls for looking after the fire, the cooking and the baby, the middle boy for catching the sods and filling the barrows, the older boy and the mother for wheeling the barrow loads out the bog. The bogs were divided in stripes about fifty yards wide so there were several families within sight of each other. Whatever anybody did, everyone knew.

In the Shannon Valley around Roscommon, Westmeath and Offaly, when the "slanesman" threw up the sods, a boy caught them and placed them on the barrow in well ordered symmetric double rows. Each row had twelve sods and weighed nearly a hundred weight. Barrow-men usually complained if more than two rows were loaded on the barrow, as the terrain was rough with clumps of caoibh and heather. In other parts of the country, the "slanesman" just threw the sods up on the bank and somebody loaded the barrow with a pitchfork in a somewhat higgledy-piggledy fashion. This was how we found things east of the Slieve Bloom Mountains near Mountrath at the end of the forties.

My uncle had bought a farm there and come April he employed a barrow-man and brought me as the turf catcher.

When I started catching the sods, work ceased on every bank and a crowd gathered. "Could I try that?" said a much older boy but the sods slipped from his grasp. You could not be up to the Connaught men, was the general consensus. This was my finest hour. Imagine a ten-year old boy being the envy of the whole bog. Could things ever get better?

Spring's Hope, Hope Springs

The windswept fields of early spring
Bereft of every living thing
Save hungry birds upon the wing
To us who hope, promises bring.

The colour from earth's cheeks has gone
The sickly sun shines pale at morn,
No lamb or bud has yet been born
The trees show nothing now but thorn.

And yet we live in hope to see
An end to all this misery,
With birds and buds on every tree,
Shade skipping lamb and buzzing bee.

The Light of Limericks

Bovril came in a small round squat jar with a screw-on lid and after the Bovril was used you could make a lamp out of the jar. All you had to do was cut a slot in the lid; insert a piece of a velour hat in the slot for a wick, put some paraffin oil in the jar, screw the lid back on, light and trim the wick and Bob's your uncle. A two-pound jam-jar with the bottom tapped out made a useable if less than presentable globe. The funny thing was that if this homemade lamp was placed high up in a room with a good reflector behind it, the light it gave was the very same as light from the most expensive lamp. Are we all equal?

Our Own

Pat Kavanagh you worked with the soil,
From dawn unto dusk you did toil.
But you turned to the pen,
'T was lucky for then
Your writing was best of them all.

Smile

Young love has a smile that has style.
Firstborn has a smile to beguile,
But with wisdom of age,
As said by the sage,
Grandchild has best smile by a mile.

Love

Love is the world's greatest treasure,
With sex it's the ultimate pleasure,
If commitments are made
Before heading to bed
And all three are used in fair measure.

Putting up the Bob

We walked three miles to school. One or two families came even further. On our way others who lived along the way joined us. Many of those came out byroads or laneways from their houses. We were always in a hurry in the mornings but it was more interesting to travel together. We could compare or even correct homework as well as giving each other encouragement against the dreaded ordeal of school with all its teasing, tests, trials and tribulations.

To aid our assembly we had a system of road markers. Every family had two marker stones that were kept at the point where they joined the road. One of those stones was for use by the main body of pupils who would put it in a particular place if they passed before the family arrived. When the family saw this they would place their own stone in place for the benefit of later comers and then they would run to catch the main bunch. The late comers would become ever more depressed and worried as the came across more and more stones neatly placed by pupils who were on time and probably had their homework well done and correct.

At this time most people had clocks but few of them had the right time. Indeed it took reasonably good scholars to estimate the right time on some of them. A conversation might go something like this; "that clock gains a little over ten minutes a day and it was put at the right time on Sunday when Big Ned was here with the American watch. It was put forward twenty minutes on Tuesday and this is Friday and it says ten past nine, so what is the right time?" If you could do that calculation correctly you would be in time for school. But then of course you probably didn't need school! The unfortunate latecomers were the very ones, who might have difficulty with the conundrum, difficulty with homework and major difficulty with the cross teacher.

Somehow, in spite of the morning worries, the days always ended and on the way home in the evenings, in much more relaxed and happy circumstances, the "bobs" were taken down and stored for the following morning. As we travelled we observed and discussed everything that happened on the farms, in the houses, in the hedgerows, in the stream, on the road, everyone we met and of course the ever changing weather. We also talked of emigration to England or America, making money and once or twice a few words about cohabitation and what might happen. We never said a word about sex, as the word had not been invented. Overall the education acquired on the way there and back was a great supplement to the book learning in school.

In spite of the long walk, the poor clothing, the black wartime bread, the cross teachers and only seven to nine years schooling, the vast majority lived long, happy and most successful lives, even adopting to different countries, climates, creeds and cultures. Indeed it was expected in the Ireland of the time that those pupils could go anywhere in the world and hold their own with the natives and they did. Are the immigrants coming here now this confident and will they be as successful? I hope so.

Avoid the Girls

Avoid the girls, his mother said,
For they will queer inside your head,
Before you know they'll have you wed,
With work and toil you'll soon be dead.

But then he met a lovely miss
And asked her for a little kiss,
Oh! Oh! He shouldn't feel like this,
Yet he can only call it bliss.

Although he thought his mind was sound
His feet just would touch the ground
His heart and head were spinning round
In ecstasy he knows he's drowned.

He knew he shouldn't feel this way
Yet thought it was his lucky day
Yes mother dear you had your say
But now, dear mother go away.

And when his wee girl gave a sigh
His heart and head were on a high,
He lost control and said Oh! My,
Now mother dear I'll say goodbye.

The Wet Battery

Over the years women's fashions have come and gone. We had skirts, long, short, mini, straight, waisted, baggy, pleated, double-pleated, box-pleated, flared, and endless others.

Men's fashions however were sometimes more weird.

After the war some ordinary people in rural Ireland started to get battery operated wireless sets. Dry batteries for those wirelesses lasted a few months but wet batteries were also required. They consisted of elements set up in a two-pint square glass jar filled with distilled water and acid. Those had to be kept upright at all times as there were ventilated at the top. They had to be recharged after every few hours use and garages with the equipment to do this were located in towns only. People cycled to the recharging depots with one hand on the handlebars and the wet battery in the other hand.

They soon became a status symbol and a girl might be heard discussing the situation as follows.

"My fellow has a wet battery."

"I didn't think he had that much spark."

"Your fellow has no battery at all."

"He doesn't need it, he runs on his own steam."

"Steam is all it is! No substance."

"It's better than having to be recharged."

"Ah but think of all you can hear on the wireless. People who have wirelesses know everything that is going on in the world and if a fellow has a wireless before he marries he will surely have one afterwards."

"That's if he hasn't spent all on batteries before that."

"It won't matter to you anyhow because he is my fellow."

Sixty years later their grandchildren are texting the following.

"My network is bigger than yours."

"My coverage is better than yours."

"My network has every boy in sixth year in the technical school."

"My coverage is able to pick up all the schools in Dublin."

"What good is a fellow a hundred miles away or are you having text drinks, text dances, text gathering or text sex? A bird in the hand is worth two in the bush."

"It would be better than some of those on your network, you are still wishful thinking, they are still in the bush and your bait is not going to bring them down. As far as you are concerned they might as well be a hundred miles away." The more things change the more they stay the same.

The River Shannon

The lordly Shannon bulges out,
It spreads its bulk upon the plain.
Through islands it works in and out,
Works out and in and out again.

It torments fishes, birds and men,
It spreads across the callow land.
It rises then recedes again,
Oh were it tame it would be grand.

'T was in the year of fifty-four
The rains came down in torrents great,
The Shannon then could hold no more,
So o'er the land it spread its weight.

It ebbed and flowed while people slept,
It crept in silent like a boat.
Up legs of chairs it slowly crept
And put men in their beds afloat.

In times before roads were good in Ireland the waterways were widely used for travel and indeed people ribbon built the waterways much as they ribbon build the roads nowadays. In the case of the river Shannon in the plains of Ireland that meant building not on the edge of the river but on the edge of the highest flood. As the land only rises gradually from the edge of the river, this meant keeping back several hundred yards and hoping that your estimate of flood limits was accurate. They seldom were as extremely wet years caught out many. Nineteen fifty four was one such year and the eighth of December was the wettest day ever remembered making it the worst year of all time.

The women having been evacuated, I was drafted in to help my uncle Tommy tending to the cattle, hens and ducks. The hens were easy as they stayed on their loft so long as they were fed; a few even provided us with fresh eggs. The ducks were more problematic as they continually tried to escape their shed to frolic in the flood where they would swim out to the deep and we would not be able to get them back. The twenty-two cattle were the big work. Of necessity, they were all tied in and they had to be fed and watered. Although they were standing in water it was fouled so we had to bucket some in from the deep, all the time wading through two feet of water. A false floor of railway planks ensured that they were above the flood level but after the sleet and rain of the 8th December the flood rose another six inches and in the morning the animals were standing in water. Another trailer load of sleepers were procured by Ferguson Twenty tractor, reversed three hundred yards to the water's edge and floated the last fifty yards to the cattle sheds. This was where the sport began. First the cow tines had to be elongated with ropes as they were anchored to the mangers. Next the animal had to be pushed around and two planks floated in on one side of her. Then the animal had to be nudged, pushed, coaxed or prodded until all four legs were on the two planks. One man held her in this position with his shoulder while the other floated in another two planks. This procedure had to be repeated with each animal.

What about living conditions? The chairs were floating in the kitchen but we had the fire up on blocks and the flitch of bacon was hanging from the roof. It never occurred to us that great pans of bacon might be bad for your health.

The bed too was on blocks and provided the daywear, the waders or socks, didn't fall off the end, one could get dressed in the morning and face another day. Who needed adventure holidays?

The Revenue Woman

Dear Mr Timothy Kelly,

It has come to our notice that you are carrying out a haulage business. We have no record of having received an income tax return from you. Please fill and return enclosed form or have your accountant contact us or call to our office personally.

PP The Revenue Commissioners.
Ann O'Reilly.

At first Timothy was mesmerised. How did those people know about him? Was it the result of the advertisement he had placed in the lonely-hearts column? He didn't know anything about the revenue commissioners but Ann O'Reilly sounded like a very nice girl. Having reached his fiftieth birthday without ever having a girlfriend, any female name sounded like a nice girl. Of course he would call to see her this very day. The town with the office was twenty miles away but not to worry, he would bring the tractor and trailer. This top-class tractor and trailer had cost over a hundred thousand euro and he was not about to hide his light under a bush. His add had read, "mature farmer with top of the range tractor and trailer seeks companion." Now he had a reply. He was not surprised. Sure that's how his schoolmate Dingo had got the wife twenty-five years ago. It was the new tractor that swung it.

Having parked his tractor and trailer he called to the open-plan revenue office. Numerous, scantily clad, beautiful creatures inhabited it. At a large desk to one side was a real mature woman, well fed and well endowed with beauty, grace and ample elegance. She totally eclipsed her hungry looking juniors. Could she possibly be Ann O'Reilly? She could, she was and she came to him smiling. She had a list of questions on a sheet of paper for him, a bit like matchmaking. This was his chance to impress her.

"Do you own a farm?"

"I do to be sure."

"How many acres?"

"Nearly thirty." It was actually twenty-five and a half and most of that was bog but he was here to impress and she was definitely interested.

"What is your weekly income?"

"The week of the Ballinasloe Fair I took in eight hundred euro for transporting cattle." She was wasting no time and he was certainly going to tell her of his earning power.

"How much of that was profit."

"Sure 'twas all profit except the cost of the diesel."

"What about depreciation."

"Sure I'm keeping fine even though I'm near forty."

"I mean repayments on the tractor."

"There's no repayments, I pay cash down for everything."

"And where did you get all this cash?"

"Oh I made a fortune with the old tractor but it was nothing to this one." He didn't mention that himself, his Father and his recently deceased brother had worked in the tannery for the last thirty-five years and that all three had saved every penny of their taxed income in a joint account. His father signed off when he qualified for the old age pension, then it was all his.

"How long had you the old tractor?"

"A good few years now."

"Would you say ten years or more?"

"About ten, sure I was only a young lad." Looking at her with her low cut white blouse, her lovely soft arms and her Oh! So kissable lips, sure he felt like a lad. He could have gone on dreaming like this forever but she meant business, she couldn't wait to know all about him. She must feel the same as him. Was this what they called love at first sight? It must be.

"And how much did you make on the old tractor in the ten years?"

"Oh a lot, enough to buy the new one and the farm and I wasn't behind the door spending a few bob either. Oh no, Timmy Kelly is no skinflint." He was on a roll, he had her in the palm of his hand, this was easier than he expected, and he might even get the whole match arranged today.

"How much did you pay for the farm?"

"Fifty-five thousand, I outbid them all."

"Have you cash in the bank?"

"Of course I have, I'm thinking of buying a car."

"What price car?"

"Ten thousand or more."

"Have you any dependents?"

"Not a one only myself for now." This girl was no flat. She wanted to make sure there was no interfering mother-in-law. How many more wonderful things would he find out about her yet? She looked him straight in the eye, smiled that dazzling smile and said, "Normally I would write to you but if you wait a few moments I will give you my preliminary findings." He wasn't sure what preliminary meant but it must be something good and it was nice that she too was in a hurry. She looked lovely at her computer. She was working some sort of calculator as well. She must be very smart and she was so sweet and soft. Wouldn't it be wonderful to just feel her? His heart missed a beat. She was coming back. "Just from a very preliminary estimate it seems you saved at least one hundred and sixty thousand euro even after living well over the last ten years. The income tax on that amount with interest and penalties comes to two hundred and forty thousand euro. I suggest you give us a cheque on account today."

"Are you telling me that I have to give you two hundred and forty thousand euro? Now look here Ann O'Reilly, you might be sweet and soft and desirable but I can't afford you, have you any cheaper models?"

Áine

Olympic winner 2003 AD

We have dreamt of mighty heroes,
For many years in Drum,
Then Áine won gold medals
And brought the bacon home.

The Olympics for the Special
Were Special from the start
And the wonder special opening,
Brought love to every heart.

Every colour, creed and race
Came here to us hand in hand,
And they cried with tears of joy
When they landed in Ireland.

Thirty thousand volunteers
Gave their talents from the start,
May God reward their efforts?
For he loves the meek of heart.

Great Ann Gately from St Hilda's
Kindly coached the special three
And their sixteen trophy medals,
Stirs the hearts of all who see.

For Aideen, Todd and Áine
Did their town and country proud,
And the bards of old Athlone,
Will now sing their praises loud.

Two Act Play
No Power on Earth
(Greedy for Land)

ACT 1
SCENE 1
An Irish farmhouse in 1960.

Three people are just returning from the funeral of the farmer, Paddy Kelly who was killed by a bull. They are his second wife Maggie, who was recently estranged and in the course of getting a legal separation and her two teenage sons, from a previous marriage, John and Pat.

The boys are scruffily dressed in very tight breeches and have bad Tony-Curtis haircuts. On stage can be seen the inside of the kitchen and a little space outside the front door.

Mother: "Now we won't have to leave here at all. I hated the thought of having to live in Arrowbawn."

She puts the kettle on the cooker.

Pat: "Only I let out the bull things would be different."

All three laugh.

Mother: "Not a minute too soon as the separation would be finalised at the end of next week. Keep your voice down now, as Peter will be here any minute."

Pat: "No he won't, his cousin Jim brought him into the pub so he'll be a while."

Mother as she makes the tea: "What exactly happened with the bull?"

Pat: "I was in the hayloft when they came in to feed him his barley and cotton-cake. Even though he was tied he was snorting at them, but he quietened down to eat before they went out. That was when I leaned down and undid his chain."

John: "What happened then, did he rush out?"

Pat: "No, only when he finished the feed did he realise he was loose and went out the door. Paddy and Peter were still in the yard and he made for them straight away. They nearly got out the gate but Paddy got squeezed against the pier. He gave a sort of squawk but he didn't seem to be badly hurt. The bull paused for a moment and Peter got both of them out and closed the gate. Tom Moran was shooting crows in the next field and he came running. Shoot him; shoot the bloody animal shouted Peter and Tom shot him between the eyes. He fell dead on the spot."

John: "What happened then?"

Pat: "Peter and Tom helped Paddy down to the house. He was moaning a bit but he could walk."

John: "They say his lungs were punctured and after a while they filled with fluid and drowned him."

Pat: "When I was in the hayloft before I let out the bull I heard them talking."

Mother has been setting the table stops and says: "Who?"

Pat: "Peter and his father, who else?"

Mother: "What about?"

Pat: "About him having a Roscommon girl up the pole."

Mother: "Are you sure, what exactly did he say?"

Pat: "He said he had this young wan expecting and when the ould fella asked him how long he said four months. The ould fella asked him how old she was and he said eighteen."

John who has his tea poured says: "Hand me the sugar."

Mother hands him the milk as she asks: "What did he say?"

Pat: "He said why didn't you tell me sooner?"

John: "That's the milk hand me the sugar."

Mother: "Here, what did he say?"

John: "Is there any butter?"

Mother: "Get the bloody butter yourself, what did he say?"

Pat: "He said he was afraid. Then the ould fella said, "are you going to marry her?" He said, "He wanted to marry her more than anything in the world, that he loved her, that he couldn't live without her."

John: "The stupid "eejit", if it was me I'd be off to England in the morning."

Mother: "Whist will ya, what did the ould fella say?"

Pat: "He said if you want to marry her she will be very welcome here. Next week when we get rid of the other three, there will be plenty of room and every house needs a woman. It's great news, great news altogether, good luck to ye."

John: "Won't he get a right land, now, that we are staying?"

Mother: " We certainly are, whether he likes it or not. Leave the talking to me, I'll put him straight about a few things."

Enter Peter; a twenty-one year old well dressed young man in coat and cap.

Peter: "Is the "tae" ready?"

Mother: "It is for us, from now on you will do your own cooking. In fact you might as well go to England as there is nothing here for you now."

Peter: "What do you mean, nothing here for me, haven't I this house and farm of land!"

Mother: "This is my house and my place."

Peter: "It's not your house."

Mother: "And who's else would it be only poor Paddy's grieving widow?"

Peter: "Grieving widow my foot. Weren't you separated and haven't you a new man?"

Mother: "That was before poor Paddy died, it's different now, the separation wasn't completed, and that's why I'm going to stay in my own house and place."

Peter: "Your house and place! Are you raving? This is my house and place now and you or your sons are not welcome. Indeed I wonder who let the bull out?"

Pat: "What do you mean?"

Peter: "I mean the bull didn't just get out himself, somebody let him out."

Pat: "You can't prove a thing."

Mother: "Keep your stupid thoughts to yourself or you'll be up for slander, not that you'll have anything to sue for after the will is read."

Peter: "What are you talking about?"

Mother: "Now Peter, things have changed, from here on you'll keep a civil tongue in your head and you'll be civil to my two lads. There are three of us and you are on your own. We might let you live on the draw-farm and leave us alone."

Peter: "I'll have you to know that this farm here has been in my family for three hundred years, our sweat and blood are in it and no power on earth will remove us from it."

Pat: "What blood?"

Peter: "After his cousin from The Flying Column was shot by The-Black-And-Tans wasn't my Grandfather arrested and tortured for a week in the military barracks in Athlone."

Mother: "The Tans were not all bad."

Peter: "Are you talking about the ones who left their seeds?"

Pat: "What do you mean? Watch your tongue."

Peter: "If the cap fits!"

Mother: "Leave that alone."

Peter: "It was ye brought it up."

Mother: "That's big talk for a lone survivor, we'll see when the will is read. The lawyer, Mr Smith will be here shortly."

Peter: "So he told me, the sooner the better."

Mother: "I didn't know he talked to you."

Peter: "So you don't know everything then, when he comes you'll learn."

Just then there is a knock, the door opens and the lawyer walks in with his briefcase. He is a man in his twenties, smartly dressed in a dark suit.

Mr Smith: "Good afternoon all, Peter will you do the introductions?"

Peter: "This is my stepmother and her sons John and Pat."

Mother: "I thought it was your father that was coming."

Mr Smith: "He is taking it a bit easier now, however, I'm sure, I'll be able to do the job. As this concerns everybody here, perhaps you would all take seats and listen."

All sit, Peter at one end of the table, Mr Smith at the other end and the mother and her two sons on one side.

Mr Smith: "This is Patrick Kelly's last will and testament."

I, Patrick Kelly, of Mulaghmore Co. Westmeath, being of sound mind, make this my last will and testament on this the eleventh day of April 1960.

Mother: "But he made the will when we married, ten years ago."

Mr Smith: "He made this will in the hospital last Monday, now listen please. To my second wife's son, John, I leave one shilling. To my second wife's other son Pat, I leave one shilling. To my second wife Maggie, I leave my draw farm at Arrowbawn together with the house thereon and my Morris-Minor motorcar, provided that she and her sons make no claim on the home farm and also that they vacate the house and farm within seven days. If they fail to honour any of those provisions, they get nothing and my entire estate goes to my only son Peter.

To my only son Peter I leave my one hundred acre home farm, complete with house and farmyard, all the livestock and machinery thereon and all remaining monies and the entire residue of my estate.

Mother: "But in the will he made ten years ago he left me everything!"

Mr Smith: "He made this will last Monday and only the last will counts."

Mother: "He couldn't have, he was too badly injured."

Mr Smith: "His injuries were to his chest, his mind was perfect."

Mother: "We will contest it in court."

Mr Smith: "That is your prerogative but you will have to get a different legal representative as I will defend this will, and remember if you fail you will lose everything."

Mother: "We'll see about that."

Mr Smith: "As my business here is complete I will take my leave. As tomorrow, Good Friday and Easter Monday are holidays perhaps you would call to see me on Tuesday Peter? Will eleven in the morning be alright?"

Peter: "Sure, I will be there at that time, I'll walk you to your car."

They both leave.

Mother: "We will have to do something. We can't just walk out of here."

Pat: "What can we do?"

Mother: "Is the bull buried?"

John: "No, we dug a huge hole in the tillage field but we will have to pull him into it with the tractor, why do you ask?"

Mother: "Wait and see."

She stands up on a chair and takes a little jar off the top of the dresser.

Pat: "Not the strychnine?"

Mother: "Why not? We'll see who will own this farm."

She pours some powder into the milk jug, stirs it and says, "Now don't either of you touch this jug."

Enter Peter and as he sits at the table says:

"Now you know who owns the place."

Mother: "All right, you win, we will be out of here by the weekend and you can bring in the "wan" you have up the pole."

Peter stops pouring his tea: "Who told you that?"

Mother: "I hear she's a right daisy."

Peter as he pours the milk:

"It's none of your business but I'll have you to know that she's a lovely girl and Daddy was delighted to hear that I was marrying her."

He drinks the tea.

Mother: "Come to live with me and you'll find out what I'm like."

Peter: "You came to live with us and I found out what you're like alright. I have a pain in my stomach."

Mother: "Here have another cup of tea."

Peter: "No I have enough."

He stands up holding his stomach, and then sits down again.

"This bloody pain is getting worse I'm going to the doctor."

Mother: "Wait a minute I'll drive you, John go up to the room and get me my coat."

John leaves.

Mother: "Is it easing any bit?"

Peter gritting his teeth: "No it's getting worse."

He lies on the couch moaning.

Mother: "John, what's keeping you? Hurry."

John comes in with the coat:

"Here it is."

As the mother puts it on Peter passes out and she takes it off again and stoops down to Peter who is now gasping loudly: "Relax Peter you'll be alright in a minute."

Peter: "Bring me to the doctor now."

Mother: "Rest for a minute, let the pain ease."

Peter gasps and stops breathing.

Mother: "I think he's gone."

Pat: "Have you killed him?"

Mother: "I hope so, hand me the mirror."

John gives her the mirror and she holds it in front of Peter.

Mother: "No breath, he's dead alright."

Pat: "He's dead! What are we going to do now?"

Mother: "Bury him and his clothes under the bull, come on, do it now. We'll say he ran to England from the Roscommon woman. Wait: Take off his topcoat and cap. I have an idea. After ye finish the burying we will drive to Portarlington to get a ticket for the boat train. Pat, you can wear his coat and cap while you are buying a ticket to London."

Pat: "I'm not going to London."

Mother: "You don't have to go to London, just buy the ticket wearing Peter's coat and cap."

Pat: "I could do that in Tullamore."

Mother: "Somebody might know you there, no it's Portarlington."

Pat and John carry out Peter.

End of scene one.

ACT ONE
SCENE TWO

The same farmhouse the following Wednesday. Mother, John and Pat are having tea at the table. Pat looks out the window.

Pat: "Mr Smith is coming again and he has Sergeant Burke with him."

Mother: "Don't worry, we'll tell them the same thing as we told the lawyer yesterday. Just stick to the story."

There is a knock at the door, Pat opens it and the Sergeant and Mr Smith walk in.

Mr Smith: "Well, did you hear from Peter since?"

Mother: "No, why should we? We told you all about him yesterday, how he had a young one in trouble and how he was not prepared to stand by her, that's why he ran away."

Mr Smith sits in a corner behind the door taking notes.

Sergeant: "Now tell me the whole story again. When did he decide to go?"

Mother: "Thursday evening, after the funeral, like I told Mr Smith yesterday, he asked me to drive him to the station in Portarlington. I said Tullamore was nearer, but he said no, people would know him there and he didn't want that. I suppose he was ashamed and so he should be after making a show of himself like that and not to have the guts to face up to his responsibilities. We all went with him in the Minor."

Sergeant: "I know, I checked it out but I'm still surprised by his timing."

Mother: "Sure he couldn't go 'till he buried his father and I suppose he was afraid the young "wan's" father would turn up with a shotgun."

Sergeant: " Do you know the girl's name?"

Mother: " No, indeed how would I? Wasn't it a secret?"

Sergeant: "How did you know about it at all?"

Mother: "Weren't they fighting about it every day for the last week!"

Sergeant: "Who?"

Mother: "Peter and Paddy, who else?"

Sergeant: "Only for a week?"

Mother: "Well maybe eight or nine days."

Sergeant: "Why eight or nine days?"

Mother: "I suppose Paddy only found out then."

Sergeant: "How did he find out?"

Mother: "How should I know, maybe Peter told him."

Sergeant: "Did Peter tell you?"

Mother: "Tell me! Are you mad? He'd rather tell the devil."

Sergeant: "So you didn't pull too well then?"

Mother: "How many young fellas tell their stepmother's about their romances even when they haven't anything to be ashamed of."

Sergeant: "What about you boys, did he say anything to either of you?"

Pat and John snigger.

Pat: "He might have."

Sergeant: "Might have what?"

Pat: "Told us what we were missing."

Sergeant: "Told you what you were missing, what do you mean?"

Pat: "You know, what he did with the woman and that, he said it was great, said he might give us a go."

Mother: "Now you know how that blackguard scandalised my lads, in jail he should be."

Sergeant: "I'm surprised that young Peter would talk that way about his girlfriend."

Mother: "Sure, he clearly didn't think much of her, or he wouldn't have spoken like that to my lads and now he's gone altogether."

Sergeant: "Did he bring the girl with him?"

The two lads look at each other.

Mother: "We didn't see her anyway but maybe she was on the train, I never thought of that."

Sergeant: "Isn't it a wonder you didn't ask him!"

Mother: "Is it me, to ask the blackguard, as if he'd tell me anyway or as if I'd care. Ask him yourself when you find him."

Sergeant: "What about you Pat, did he tell you if the girl was on the train?"

Pat: "Not a word about her, if you ask me he was running away from her."

Sergeant: "John, did he say anything to you?"

John: "Not a word, only about letting us have a go."

Sergeant: "When was that?"

John looks at his mother.

Pat: "He told us last week."

Sergeant: "I'm not talking to you, John, answer my question."

John: "He told us last week like Pat said, why are you asking me?"

Sergeant: "I am asking you, what day did he tell you?"

Pat: "He was talking about her for a long time."

Sergeant: "For the last time I'm telling you to keep out of this, John when did he tell you?"

John: "Like he said he was always talking about her."

Sergeant: "What was he saying about her?"

John: "You know."

Sergeant: " No I don't know, you tell me what was he saying about her?"

John: "That she was a good thing and that he would give us a go."

Sergeant: "Are you absolutely certain of that? Did he ever say her name?

John: "No."

Sergeant: "What did he call her?"

John: "I don't know, I wasn't there."

Sergeant: "This whole thing seems suspicious, would you like to come down to the station with me John to make a statement?"

John looks at his Mother, who says, "Why would you want him down at the station? Talk to him here."

John: "I didn't do anything."

Sergeant: "We're not accusing you of anything, we just want to ask you a few questions."

Mother: "Ask them here. You have no right to be hounding my child like that."

Sergeant: "There's a man dead and another man missing I have every right to ask questions of whoever I see fit."

Mother: "Is it what you think Peter killed his father? Indeed I wouldn't put it past him."

Sergeant: "I think nothing of the sort now stop interrupting my conversation with John."

There is a knock at the door, Mr Smith opens it and a young girl, obviously pregnant, comes in and asks,

"Is Peter Kelly here?"

Mr Smith gently asks: "Who are you?"

"I'm Kitty Reilly, Peter's girlfriend, is he here?"

Mother: "No, he's gone to England, gone and left you."

Kitty: "I don't believe you, Peter would never leave me."

Sergeant: "When did you see him last?"

Kitty: "Last Sunday week, he was to call Saturday but he sent a telegram saying his father was killed and that he would call to see me as soon as possible, where is he?"

Mr Smith: "Sit down here."

Mother: "He's gone to England like I told you. I left him to the train myself."

Kitty bursts into tears.

Mother: "Stop your whinging, you're lucky to miss him, he's not worth much, ran away when he had the harm done. Now everybody knows what he's like. Are you surprised now Mr Smith?"

Mr Smith tries to console Kitty, who is now hysterical and says:

"Leave the girl alone."

Kitty: "What is to become of me now, where will I go?"

Mr Smith: "Don't worry now, my wife and I will look after you?"

Mother to Sergeant: "Now do you believe me that he went to England? Now, you know why, the dirty blackguard, I told you didn't I?"

Sergeant to Mr Smith: "Our business here is finished for now, come I want a few words with you outside."

The Sergeant, Mr Smith and Kitty leave. Outside the door the sergeant asks Kitty,

"Tell me again, when was the last time you saw Peter?"

Kitty still sobbing: "Last Sunday week, he said we would get married as soon as he told his father about me. He said that one day we would build a new house out near the road overlooking the lake."

Sergeant: "Did his father not know about you?"

Kitty: "He knew about me but not about, about."

Sergeant: "About the pregnancy?"

Kitty: "Yes, he didn't know that, Peter was to tell him last week."

Sergeant: "Did he tell him?"

Kitty: "I don't know, he didn't say in the telegram."

Sergeant: "Was he to tell him before?"

Kitty: "He was, but he was afraid his father would be vexed."

Sergeant: "Why would he tell him this week, when he hadn't told him before?"

Kitty: "Because I couldn't keep it hid any longer, now what am I going to do?"

Mr Smith: "Like I said you will come home with me, my wife will look after you."

Sergeant: "Are you absolutely certain you did not hear from Peter since Sunday week?"

Kitty: "Certain."

Sergeant: "Does your family know about Peter and you?"

Kitty: "They know about Peter but not about, you know."

Sergeant: "Not about the pregnancy."

Kitty: "No they don't know about that, my father would kill me or Peter or both, what am I going to do?"

Mr Smith: "Like I said, come home with me and Fidelma will look after you. Stop crying and don't worry about a thing."

Sergeant: "You know Kitty I think that's a very good idea, Mr Smith and his wife are a lovely couple and it's a good offer."

Kitty: "Thanks very much, I will go so."

Sergeant to Mr Smith: "The whole story sounds more believable now, don't you think?"

Mr Smith: "It looks that way but something seems wrong. Peter was very sure of coming to see me on Tuesday. I wonder what changed his mind? Kitty, are you sure your father didn't find out?"

Kitty: "No, no, sure he would have said it to me, he would have gone mad."

Mr Smith: "Maybe, he found out and came to see Peter, before saying anything to you?"

Kitty: "You don't know my father, he loses the head first and thinks later, he'd have my guts for garters first and he'd deal with Peter after."

Mr Smith: "Have you any brothers that might have found out?"

Kitty: "Sure my brothers are only "laddeens", the five oldest are girls and I am the oldest. That's what makes it so bad, I have a show made of them all, now every chancer will think my young sisters are easy touches and worse, Peter is gone."

Mr Smith: "It seems we can do no more for now only look after this poor girl."

Sergeant: "It looks that way so I will say goodbye, goodbye Kitty and don't worry you're in good hands."

All three leave.

End of Act One.

ACT TWO

The same farmhouse forty-five years later, 2005. The mother, who is now a witch-like old woman is in her badly kept bed in the kitchen where she moved it some months ago when her room began to leak. Pat and John are decrepit old men. Where the old wireless was before there is now an old television. An overgrown hedge now obscures the front door.

John: "I knew the new road would bring no luck."

Pat: "What are you talking about? Aren't they paying good money?"

John: "Peter did say that no power on earth could move his family from this farm."

Pat: "Well he was wrong wasn't he? The roads crowd dug him up and the coroner took him away, we're well rid of him."

John: "The money won't be much good if they find out who's the bones are that they found under the bull."

Mother: "How would they find out after all this time? And even if they did it has nothing to do with us, it could have been the slut's father or brothers."
John: "Who told you that she had a father and brothers?"
Mother: "Nobody told me she hadn't and anyway he probably had other enemies. Maybe she had other fellas? It has nothing to do with us."
John: "I wonder was Sergeant Flynn satisfied with what we said yesterday?"
Pat: "Why wouldn't he be, sure we can't be expected to know who might be buried on the land."
John: "They will surely know how long he is dead and then they will suspect it is Peter."
Pat: "Not at all, you are worrying about nothing. Sure Sergeant Burke is dead this twenty years and he never met Sergeant Flynn."
John looking out the window: "The Sergeant and old Mr Smith are outside."
There is a knock at the door, Pat opens it and the Sergeant and Mr Smith come in. Mr Smith sits behind the door and the Sergeant says,

"Just to clear things up you might answer another few questions. Have any of you any idea who the man we found might be?"
Pat: "We were just talking about it and we have no idea. Have you any idea how long was he there?"
Sergeant: "We're working on it, we should know soon. There was an animal buried with him, would any of you know anything about that?"
Pat: "Wasn't that very strange? Sure they must be there since "Ould God's" time."
Sergeant: "Paddy Kelly was killed by a bull and a neighbour shot the bull, is that right?"
Pat: "That's right but what has that to do with this?"
Sergeant: "Where was the bull buried?"
Pat: "In the tillage field."
Sergeant: "Where the bones were found?"
Pat: "Ah no, as far as I remember it was well down the field, the bones were found near the gate."
Sergeant: "Who dug the hole?"

Pat: "We did, with Peter and a big job it was but there was nothing buried there but the bull."

Sergeant: "How did you get the bull into the hole?"

Pat: "Peter pulled him in with the tractor."

Sergeant: "Are you sure it was Peter?"

Pat: "It was, sure no one else could drive the tractor at that time."

Sergeant: "Were ye with him?"

Pat: "We weren't too far away but he did it on his own and filled it in with the transport box."

Sergeant: "Was there anything in the hole before the bull?"

Pat: "We didn't see anything"

Sergeant: "Did ye look?"

Pat: "Not that I remember, why would we?"

Sergeant: "Could there have been a body there unknown to you?"

Pat: "We didn't see it anyway."

Sergeant: "Could it have been there?"

Pat: "If it was covered with clay maybe."

Sergeant: "John did you see anything?"

Mother: "Wouldn't it be more in your line to be out looking for the blackguards who are robbing and killing old people in their own homes than hounding decent people about old bones! Sure when the lads are out at night aren't I in fear for my life or worse?"

Sergeant: "John did you see anything in the hole?"

John: "Only the bull like Pat said."

Sergeant: "Where was the hole exactly?"

John: "Down the field like Pat said."

Sergeant: "Do you remember anything yourself only what Pat remembers?"

Pat: "Didn't you say the bones were there since old times?"

Sergeant: "Preliminary investigations by our experts suggest they were there less than fifty years."

John: "How could they know that?"

Sergeant: "We have great ways now, indeed when we get the DNA results we may even know who he was."

John: "How could you possibly know who he was, sure there was nothing there only bones."

Sergeant: "There's more to bones than you might think, we'll see when we get the results."

John: "When will you get them?"

Sergeant: "Very soon I hope."

John: "But you still won't have a name?"

Sergeant: "We should know if he belonged to any family round here and from there we should be able to deduce who he was."

John: "How could you do that?"

Sergeant: "We have our ways, now for instance if the skeleton was that of Peter Kelly it would match with his cousin's DNA."

John and Pat: "What makes you think it is Peter?"

Mother: "Didn't Peter run to England, it couldn't be him anyway."

Sergeant: "I didn't say it was Peter but ye seem to think it is. I wonder why?"

Mother: "Maybe the young "wan's" father came after Peter and maybe Peter killed him and threw him in the hole, did you ever think of that? Did you? And then he ran to England. If ye were doing your job you'd bring him back and make him face the music."

There is a knock at the door, Pat opens it and "Peter" still young, walks in dressed in very good modern casual clothes. Pat recoils in fright to his screaming mother. John does likewise.

Mother, John and Pat wail: "Peter!"

Mother: "You're back, back to haunt us."

"Peter" just points a finger at the old woman and says: "You."

Mother very distraught and frightened: "I'm sorry, I'm sorry I poisoned you, sure we never had a day's luck since."

Pat: "Shut up mother, this is a trick, who the hell are you?"

"Peter": "So you were in on it too, what did you do? Bury the body?"

John: "He knows it all, why wouldn't he? Wasn't it to him we did it and his father when you let out the bull?"

The sergeant grabs Pat and handcuffs him to his mother and does the same with John. He then turns to "Peter" and asks: "Who are you?"

Peter: "My name is Paul Quinn, I'm a molecular geneticist with the Royal Academy in London. Your colleagues sent two samples for DNA testing, one from the skeleton of forty-five years ago and the other from a person who might be his cousin. The two were definitely related but there was something else much more important."

Sergeant: "What could be more important?"

Paul: "The dead man was my direct ancestor and from his age he has to be my grandfather, that is why I came here direct with the result."

Mother: "You're not Peter, you tricked us."

John: "He did say no power on earth would part them from their land."

Pat: "Shut up you fool!"

John: "Fool is it? Who got us into this mess?"

He holds up the handcuffs.

Paul looks around and sees Mr Smith. In great surprise he says, "Granddad! What are you doing here? Are there some things I should know?"

Mr Smith: "There are indeed. After your real granddad disappeared your real grandmother turned up here looking for him. She was pregnant and was devastated when she heard he was gone. Although we were only married two years, my late wife Fidelma, just had a disastrous miscarriage and was told she could never have children as a result. I decided to bring your grandmother home to Fidelma to see if we could help her. Fidelma was delighted to help. We sent your grandmother to my sister in Dublin for the remainder of her time, when she had a baby girl, your mother. At that time it was almost impossible for an unmarried girl to rear a child in Ireland so she decided to give her baby for adoption. She left the arrangements to my sister and we adopted the baby. Your mother never knew she was adopted and as you know, Fidelma treasured her up to the day she died. With Fidelma gone, your mother in Galway and you in London Its very lonely round here."

Paul: "Am I related to those three?"

Mr Smith: "No, not at all, she was Paddy Kelly's second wife and she came with these two sons, he had only one child of his own, your granddad. In fact I would be of the opinion now that you are the rightful heir to this place."

There is a knock at the door and the sergeant opens it.

Sergeant: "Mammy! Err Kitty, What are you doing here?"

Kitty: "I read on the paper that there was a body found on this farm. I think I might know who it is." *Just then she spots Paul and shouts:* "Peter" *and faints into the arms of Mr Smith who puts her sitting in his chair and holds her in position with his hands on her shoulders. She slowly recovers.*

Paul: "It seems everybody round here knows who I am except me."

Sergeant to Kitty: "Are you alright?"

Kitty: "I am, I am, I just got a fright there for a minute." *Looking at Paul she says:* "You have to be related to Peter, how?"

Paul: "It seems I'm his grandson, who are you?"

Kitty: "In that case it seems I'm your grandmother."

Paul is dumbfounded and just stares.

Sergeant: "Mam, Err Kitty what are you saying?"

Kitty: "I'm saying that Peter and I had a beautiful baby girl but he disappeared before we could get married and I had to give her up for adoption."

Sergeant: "Did Daddy know this?"

Kitty: "I told him all about it the first night we met, in Ballygar carnival it was. He never mentioned it again up to the day he died two years ago."

Mr Smith: "Well Kitty you look great, life must have been kind to you. Do you remember me?"

Kitty looking up at him places her hands on his and says: "Mr Smith! The kindest person I ever knew. How is your wonderful wife Fidelma?"

Mr Smith: "Gone to her eternal reward two years ago."

Kitty: "I'm so sorry."

She turns to Paul without letting go Mr Smith's hands:

"And what is your name and where is your mother?"

Paul: "My name is Paul and my mother should be here any time now. I rang her on the mobile and told her I was visiting my ancestor's grave; she was totally amazed and said she would be on her way in five minutes. This morning I had just one Grandfather but now I am acquiring grandparents and relations at an alarming speed, I could get used to this."

Mr Smith: "And land."

Paul: "Right-on! There's a lovely site overlooking the lake, is that part of the estate?"

Mr Smith: "It is indeed."

Paul: "I wouldn't mind building a house there."

Kitty: "That's where Peter was going to build a house for us."

Sergeant: "We all seem to be acquiring extra family."

He holds out his hand to Paul and says:

"Put it there brother or is it nephew?"

Paul: "It's nephew I think."

There is a knock at the door. The sergeant opens it and a glamorous forty-something year old lady walks in.

Paul: "Mum, you made it!"

Mum: "Paul! Dad! Is this some sort of family reunion?"

Paul: "Much more than you know Mum! Much more than you know!"

Final Curtain.

Glossary

A Gra: Little love.
Bob: Shilling.
Ban Garda: Policewomen.
Black-and-Tans: Auxiliary British Police.
Children's Allowance: State subvention paid for children.
Chreature: Illicit whiskey.
Cluiche Peil: Gaelic football.
Camán: Hurley stick.
Craic: Party sport.
Culchie: Rustic country person.
Droppeen: Small amount of liquid, tincture, "a few gallons".
Down: Soft under feathers on geese.
Fags: Cigarettes.
Flail: Hand operated threshing tool.
GAA: Gaelic Athletic Association.
Gossen: Boy.
Go hiontach: Wonderful.
Go halainn: Grand.
High Nellie: Pre war bicycle.
Laddeens: Small boys.
Luas: Dublin light rail system.
Leabaigh: Old Irish for bed.
Moryagh: My foot!
Pale: British area around Dublin.
Parlour: Sitting room.
Peelers: British police.
Poteen: Illicit whiskey.
Sassenach: English.
Shimmies: White linen nightgown, made from flour sacks, worn by poor Irish women and children.
Siege of Ennis: Fast Irish dance.
Slither: Hurling ball.
Soot Drop: A sooty raindrop that came down the chimney.
Sugan chair: Straw, rope and timber chair.
Tae: Tea.
Twig: Old type sweeping brush.
Viceroy: British Ruler in Ireland.